QUIETLY, LOVING EVERYONE

Quietly, Loving Everyone

CURTIS JOHN MCRAE

Stories

ESPLANADE BOOKS
THE FICTION IMPRINT AT VÉHICULE PRESS

Published with the generous assistance of the Canada Council for the Arts, the Canada Book Fund of the Department of Canadian Heritage, and the Société de développement des entreprises culturelles du Québec (SODEC).

Canada SODEC Québec

Canada Council for the Arts Conseil des arts du Canada

Esplanade Books editor: Dimitri Nasrallah
Cover design: David Drummond
Typeset in Minion and Filosofia by Simon Garamond
Printed by Marquis Imprimeur

Dépôt légal, Library and Archives Canada and Bibliothèque nationale du Québec, second quarter 2025

Library and Archives Canada Cataloguing in Publication

Title: Quietly, loving everyone : stories / Curtis John McRae.
Names: McRae, Curtis John, author.
Identifiers: Canadiana (print) 20250134640 | Canadiana (ebook) 2025014137X | ISBN 9781550656756 (softcover) | ISBN 9781550656800 (EPUB)
Subjects: LCGFT: Short stories.
Classification: LCC PS8625.R328 Q54 2025 | DDC C813/.6—dc23

Published by Véhicule Press, Montréal, Québec, Canada

Distribution in Canada by LitDistCo
www.litdistco.ca

Distribution in US by Independent Publishers Group
www.ipgbook.com

Printed in Canada on FSC certified paper.

For my mother,
Lynn Wilson

Contents

Loving birds is easy,
Any fool can do it,
But I must admit it's
Hard to love the louse.

–W.H. AUDEN, "Heavy Date"

Hotel Viviane

THE WORST PART was the feeling that it would never stop. Viviane squinted, looking like she might sneeze for an eleventh time, but really she was trying not to cry.

It was her brothers' favourite game. Cliff—fifteen and the oldest of the three-brother platoon—flicked Viviane's nose and they counted how many times she sneezed. They'd waited until Viviane had gone out to play in the backyard, where they corralled her into the shed and held her against the dirt floor.

"Flick it again." Judd looked up at Cliff wide-eyed, restraining Viviane's ankles. He had buck teeth and freckles and had earned his post as second-in-command through age alone.

"It's against the rules," Cliff said. "Only one flick. Hold her tighter or she'll squirm away."

Viviane wriggled in the dirt, twisting to free herself. Cliff was almost twice her age and sat astride her chest. He only needed to rest a bit more weight on her, but instead grinned and pinned her arms down with his knees. His kneecaps bit into her arms like incisors. Viviane winced, squeezing her eyes shut and trying not to cry.

"Enemy reinforcements?" Cliff looked over his shoulder, checking in with Norm at the window.

Most of the blinds were shut. Norm strained to detect any movement through the windows. He knew if their mother ever caught them, she would hang them by their collars from the clothesline.

"Negative," Norm replied, peering through pretend binoculars.

Norm and Judd were twins. They wore matching denim overalls with no T-shirts underneath. Both thirteen, Norm was born only a few minutes after Judd—a fact neither brother let him forget. Being the youngest, Norm was always relegated to lookout duty.

"She's at ten!" Judd belched, still holding her legs. They all knew the significance of ten. Judd peeped up at Norm now, who mirrored the same buck-toothed grin.

Viviane's head fell back, her nose scrunched up, and they all watched attentively. Norm abandoned his post to catch a glimpse of the excitement. They crowded around her. Viviane felt a volley of hands pinning her to the ground, and worried they were ruining her dress.

She drew in a breath of air.

"*Eleven! Eleven!*"

The boys trampled around and kicked up a cloud of dust that floated upward in the beams of light, spilling in through cracks in the old tin roof. "*A new record!*" The platoon scurried out from the shed, funneling into the backyard through the wooden doorframe. In the sunlight, they scattered like excited particles across the yard.

In the shed, Viviane pushed herself up from the ground. She was relieved that the feeling she had once worried might not leave her—this never-ending sneezing—had presently come to a halt. Now that she could see again, she realized that her white dress was ruined. Dirt was smeared across the back and the purple ribbon tied around the waist had torn.

Viviane wished she could hit her brothers with a baseball bat for ruining her dress. She wanted to watch bigger boys pin them to the ground and give them wet willies and torture them, but what she really wanted was to be bigger and older so she could fight back, defend herself.

The boys leapt around the yard, failing to notice the blind slats that were pinched together and the set of eyes peering out from behind them. No one was on lookout, not even Norm. The back door swung open and nearly fell off its hinges. Joy stood on the porch.

"*All* of you, get over here *now!*" Joy placed Viviane's suitcase at her feet and leaned on the railing to walk down the porch steps.

The boys hopped over the chain-link fence that lined the yard. Cliff had the longest legs, but with the threat of punishment, they all ran fast. They were halfway down the block when Viviane finally emerged from the shed with her head hung.

"What have you done to your dress? Don't you know I borrowed that from the Websters? We have to return that after your trip."

"It wasn't my fault."

"It never is."

"The boys flicked my nose again."

"Stop *sniveling*, would you? I'm going to have to pay for dry cleaning." Joy was economical in every way; she rolled her pennies, redeemed coupons scissored out of grocery store brochures, and even gave her children monosyllabic names. Viviane was the only exception.

Viviane wiped her tears away with the backs of her hands then balled them into fists. Closing her eyes, she used her whole body to try and stop herself from crying. Viviane had been looking forward to this trip with her sister. She hadn't seen Rose in weeks and was excited to surprise her with the new dress that Joy had borrowed for her. The whole thing was ruined now, and she couldn't help but feel the trip was spoiled too.

"Come here now." Joy waved her hand. "Rose is going to be here any minute."

Joy steadied Viviane with one arm and beat the dress like a dusty rug with the other. Viviane didn't squirm or twist her way out; she remained limp, submitting to that same helpless feeling, hoping it might work and the dirt might come off.

"That'll have to do. Your sister's here."

Joy patted Viviane as Rose's janky yellow car lurched forward, then came to an abrupt halt in the driveway. The car was a second-hand 1982 two-door Volkswagen Jetta, a gift Rose's stepdad Joseph had gotten her as a going away gift. It was ten years old, two years older than Viviane, and Joseph liked to joke that it was the fifth-oldest child, which made Viviane feel even younger than she already did. Rose rolled down the car window.

"I've come to collect a Viviane!" she shouted. Rose opened the car door and ran up the driveway.

"Hello to you *too*," Joy said.

"It's good to see you, Mom." Rose kissed her mother on the cheek.

"I still don't understand the need to steal your sister away and bring her to *Massachusetts*."

"We already talked about this on the phone, Mom." Rose glanced down at her sister. "I won't always be around to show her how to live."

"Don't talk like that. It upsets me."

"Oh, it's a figure of speech. I'll live forever."

Rose wrapped Viviane up. "How's my favourite sister?"

"I'm your only sister."

"You're growing up too quickly." Rose held Viviane at arm's length now. "Would you slow down?"

Joy left the sisters to chat and carried Viviane's suitcase toward the car.

Before leaving for university in Montreal, Rose had warned Viviane that anything happening on the South Shore wasn't really life, but a slow procession of imitations. In their two-storey house, with each wasted second, something greater and adjacent was passing them by. Rose had phoned a couple weeks earlier to tell Viviane she was returning to smuggle her out of Greenfield Park, to show her a glimpse of this parallel life. During their call, Rose said she hoped Viviane might move away from the South Shore one day. Viviane pretended to know why.

"Can I know where we're going now?" Viviane asked.

"Cape Cod, Massachusetts!" This fell flat, so Rose carried on. "To go and see Race Point Lighthouse."

"A lighthouse?" Viviane wasn't going to mention that she had no idea where Massachusetts was.

"That's right."

"So that boats don't get lost."

"You're too clever," Rose said.

For the first time all morning, Viviane felt like she could smile.

"I got a new dress."

"I saw. Pretty, isn't it? A little dirty though."

"They flicked my nose again."

"Don't let them bother you. They're just jealous that you get to go on a road trip." Rose looked up in Joy's direction, then back down at Viviane. "Can I trust you with a secret?"

Viviane followed her sister's gaze, double-checking that the person the secret was meant to be kept from wasn't looking.

"I promise I won't tell."

Rose's hair was shoulder length, and when she tucked a few strands behind her ear, Viviane leaned toward her.

"You have a hole in your ear?" Viviane had never seen this and didn't quite understand what she was looking at.

"It's an earring. It's called a spacer," Rose clarified.

"Does it hurt?"

"No."

"Can I get one?"

"Are you kidding? Mom would have my head. Don't tell her, okay?"

She held her pinky out, and Viviane wrapped her finger around her older sister's.

"Do you like it?"

"Yes," she lied.

Now that the car was packed, Joy returned to see her daughters off. "You remember what I told you?" She was fiddling with something in her pocket.

"No fun to be had at any time?"

"I wrote it all in a list. Here, take it." She handed over an envelope. "I packed a few lunches. Don't eat too much junk food, have Viviane in bed by ten, and don't leave the hotel after dark. Do you hear me?"

Rose pulled out a folded piece of paper, then sifted through what was left in the envelope.

"I can't take this."

Joy waved her off. "I won't hear of it."

"I told you I've been working, and I sold my art supplies."

"Which I don't understand how you're doing while studying. You know, if you ever want to come back home…"

"Mom. We've talked about this."

"I worry about you. You're stubborn."

"I wonder where I get it from." Rose glanced over and stuck her tongue out at Viviane.

"Just take it."

Rose pocketed the envelope and saluted her mother.

"Aye, aye, Captain. We'll call you when we get there, and every night. And we'll see you soon."

"So, she *does* listen."

Viviane climbed into the passenger seat of the car, and as they pulled out of the driveway, Joy waved goodbye from the porch. Looking out from the back window, Viviane watched as her house and her mother got smaller and smaller the farther they drove away.

For a moment, Viviane missed her brothers, but that feeling left just as quick as it came. There was a charge in the air, and Viviane felt like she was seeing everything for the first time. Being on the road felt like what she imagined it would feel like to drink a cup of coffee. The radio blared "I Will Always Love You" by Whitney Houston and Rose belted out the lyrics, steering with one hand.

"Roll your window down." Rose lowered the radio and pointed toward a field of cows.

"Why?" Viviane was more concerned with a sign they were passing, which read *Milton, Vermont.*

"We're going to play a game."

"What is it?"

"We'll take turns sticking our heads out the window and yelling, '*hey cow.*' Whoever turns more cow heads wins."

Viviane had to unbuckle her seatbelt to get her head out the window, and as they passed the field, she leaned out of the car and yelled louder than she thought she could. With the wind whipping her hair and the rolling cumulus clouds, she completely forgot about her brothers and the dirt on her dress. When she did remember it, she decided she liked that her dress was a little dirty. It looked like she had just been rolling around in a field of cows. That's what people like Rose did, Viviane thought; they went on road trips and wore dirty clothes, they yelled at cows and stuck their heads out of car windows, they opened themselves up to the world and stretched holes in their ears. What they didn't do, Viviane was now certain, was cry when their brothers flicked their nose.

Viviane lost track after counting twenty-two cows. She lowered herself back into her seat and turned to Rose.

"Now it's your turn."

Rose was staring ahead through the windshield.

"Rose?" Viviane poked her older sister, who moved as if roused from a dream. Rose looked over at her with a faint smile.

"He used to take me there."

"Who did?"

"Your dad, before you were born. He'd take me to the lighthouse, and we played this game together."

"Oh." Viviane wondered if her dad had ever gotten more than twenty-two.

"It's your turn now."

"I'm not even going to try. You take that round." Rose turned up the radio and let the music fill the car.

They rolled their windows down again along the coast, only this time there were no cows. Viviane had tasted salt before—Joy's pork chops and the canned sardines she made her eat—but she had never smelled saltwater, which was light but also heavy. It made the air lighter, like she could breathe more of it in, but she felt the salt on her skin, which made her feel heavier in the seat of the car.

"I've got one more secret for you," Rose said, "before we visit the lighthouse tomorrow."

"I can stretch a hole in my ear?"

"Not a chance, but look."

They pulled up to the entrance of their hotel, where a doorman in a funny red coat and matching hat awaited them beside the sliding glass doors. Above, a grand marquee with a row of large round light bulbs, and in bolded black letters, a sign that read *HOTEL VIVIANE.*

"They've been expecting you." Rose pointed up to the sign.

"Is that for me?" Viviane couldn't understand how Rose had planned this, and not once did it cross her mind that there may have already been a hotel with her name. She looked at her older sister and wondered how she had so many secrets, how she seemed to understand everything, how she was brave enough to move away from home, and how, in those puzzling ways the world opens up to you when you do the same, she was able to accomplish anything, like having an entire hotel named after her younger sister.

Rose parked abruptly, then ran around the car to greet the doorman and whisper something into his ear. Viviane watched him nod, then open her door and bow as she hopped out onto the sidewalk.

"Good evening, Ms. Viviane. We've been expecting you. Let me bring your suitcases to your room."

Viviane would have liked to pinch the sides of her soiled white dress and curtsy, but she was embarrassed, and instead of curtsying, she found herself blushing and wondering how they could afford to stay in such a fancy hotel. That morning, when she was pinned against the ground, she could have never dreamed that such a pretty building would be named after her. In the lobby, receptionists occupied a large marble counter where people checked into their rooms, and there was a swanky bar where the two of them ate dinner after several minutes of Rose discussing something with the hostess.

"What happened?" Viviane asked as they made their way to their table.

"They weren't going to let us in, since you're underage," Rose said, looking around the bar. "And I didn't want to embarrass her. She didn't realize that you were *the* Viviane."

The bar had ornate sconces fixed to the walls and tall white candles at each table, so that Viviane's dress finally looked clean in the dim lighting. Spines of wax dripped down the sides of the candles and were caught by a saucer at the bottom of the holder. There were open floor-to-ceiling windows looking out at the ocean. The flames flickered in the breeze, casting shadows across the white tablecloths. On a circular stage in the middle of the restaurant, a man in a white suit played a black baby grand piano. Somehow, the room felt like another secret to Viviane, and she thought about how she would keep this whole trip, along with everything that Rose had told her, a secret for the rest of her life.

"What do you want to eat?"

"A hamburger." Viviane held the menu with both hands, then placed it down on the table.

"Are you sure? They have steak and fancy fish here…"

"A hamburger with no toppings. Raw onions repeat themselves on me."

"Where did you hear that?"

"I heard Mom say it after belching," Viviane spoke to Rose, but her eyes wandered the room.

At the adjacent table, a man with golden rings sat on the same side of the table as a man with a pearl necklace. Viviane watched them, their fingers intertwined, then looked to Rose to see if she noticed this too, or if it was worth noticing. She had never seen two men hold hands. During recess one day, a group of boys had tried to get Viviane and her best friend Mathilda to kiss. Viviane wouldn't have minded kissing Mathilda, she had even wondered what it would be like, but she hadn't wanted to give the boys what they wanted, so she didn't. Unaware that she was staring, Viviane watched and hoped the two men might kiss. Then she could go home and tell Mathilda what she had seen, and maybe they could try it too. One of the men turned toward Viviane and winked at her.

"Viviane," Rose said with a smile. "You're staring."

"Sorry." She blushed, which was hardly noticeable in the light, but the man smiled and blew her a kiss.

While eating her burger, Viviane felt older knowing that she was learning something about the world that her friends in Greenfield Park didn't know. If those boys kept teasing her and Mathilda at recess, she would tell them that there was a hotel named after her, and that she had an older sister who knew a lot of things about the world, and that when you left the South Shore, there were places where men liked to hold hands.

They went to their room after dinner and Rose let Viviane watch TV until 10:45 p.m. As Viviane's eyes began to feel heavy, Rose turned the TV off with the remote and whispered goodnight into the dark room. Viviane was already fast asleep.

In a pink one-piece bathing suit with white trim and yellow polka dots, Viviane looked up at the foot of Race Point Lighthouse.

She squinted. "I don't see him."

"He's up there," Rose said. "Look closer."

The lighthouse towered above them, blocking out the sun while reminding Viviane of her brothers.

"I still don't see him," she said.

"Maybe he's hiding. I heard he's shy." Rose took her sister's hand and walked toward the beach.

Beneath their feet, the smooth concrete footpath turned to gravel, then to sand. The seagulls circling overhead were twice the size of any she had seen in Greenfield Park, and they flew much closer, too. They didn't seem to be afraid, and Viviane tried to do the same.

"He's not used to seeing people. He lives there year-round and isn't allowed to come down."

"Why not?"

"Because if he did, the boats might get lost."

"Then how does he eat?"

"You see those seagulls over there?"

"Those?" Viviane pointed, pretending she was seeing them for the first time.

"They collect food from the beach and bring it up to him. Sometimes they even steal bagels from little girls' hands."

"Doesn't he get lonely?" Viviane asked.

"He has the birds and the ocean."

"And he can never come down?"

"Not until he's replaced."

"By who?"

"Well, you're looking at her."

"You?" Viviane stopped walking and kneeled down to bury her hands in the sand.

"That's right. I'll be moving here to live in the lighthouse."

"What about school?"

"I dropped out."

"I don't believe you," Viviane said while grabbing fistfuls of sand and letting them fall over her feet, forming little piles.

"I really did."

Viviane felt like sneezing and didn't want to walk anymore. She sat down and crossed her arms. Rose walked a few steps farther, then turned around and approached her sister.

"You'll be able to visit me."

"But you're not allowed down."

"I never said you couldn't come up," Rose said.

"But you're already gone. Now you'll be even further."

Rose smiled at Viviane, but her smile appeared both light and heavy, like the salt on her skin. Viviane had also never seen her older sister look so sad.

"I'm here, aren't I? I brought you here, didn't I?"

The seagulls circled overhead and Viviane mindlessly ran her fingers through the sand. Rose was sitting beside her now.

"Can I bring my friend Mathilda?" Viviane asked.

"Only her."

Viviane pulled her hands out from the sand so she could scratch her nose. She didn't feel like she had to sneeze anymore.

"*Look.*" Rose pointed up to the lighthouse. "I just saw him. Did you see him too?"

"Yes, he waved at me." Viviane wasn't sure if this was a lie. The white water broke against the shore and lapped up in foam before retreating.

"Are you ready to swim now?"

Viviane jumped up and raced toward the water, knowing her sister would soon follow. She was the fastest runner in her grade, but in the soft sand the ground sunk beneath her feet with each slowed stride. Once she was waist-deep, the water knocked Viviane down with every wave. She didn't mind being knocked down; it even made her laugh. Rose fell with Viviane each time she fell. Then she picked her up and held her in her arms. Viviane's toes touched the surface of the water, the splash from the ocean sprayed her shins, and nothing about it made her feel helpless.

They walked back to shore and Viviane was sure she saw the lighthouse keeper now. He swiftly crossed the galley deck like a shadow, tall and slender, and then he disappeared into the lighthouse. She didn't see anything else, but sensed he was as much an apparition as a human, that he was only a placeholder that would soon be replaced by her sister. She hoped her sister would stay longer, and wouldn't pass like a shadow.

When they sat back down on the beach, Viviane sang a song that came into her head because she was thinking of home.

They built the ship Titanic,
To sail the ocean blue,
They thought they had a ship,
That the water would never go through,
But the good Lord raised his hand,
That the ship would never land,
It was sad when the great ship went down.
Husbands and wives,
Little children lost their lives,
It was sad when the great ship went down.

"That's a terrible song. Where did you learn that?" Rose said, looking at her.

"Me and Mathilda learned it at school."

"They teach you that?"

"No, some of the boys did."

"It's a horrible song. You shouldn't sing that."

"Why, is it bad?" Viviane asked.

"It's about people dying."

"Oh." She had thought it was catchy. The ocean had made her think of it.

Rose sat in silence for a while.

"Why don't you go and dig for sand dollars? Then you can bring some home for Mom."

"Where will you be?"

"I'll just be sitting over here."

So Viviane did; she dug for sand dollars, cleaning her hands and toes in the ocean between each find, occasionally getting knocked over by a wave and laughing. Whenever she looked over at the beach to see if her sister was still there, Rose waved. She was watching Viviane, but she also seemed to be looking past her. Viviane worried that Rose might sink into the sand, or else get up and wander off, leaving her behind. She kept checking to make sure her sister was there. She couldn't understand why Rose would be sad. Rose was going to live in the lighthouse soon, which was what she wanted.

Viviane decided that twenty sand dollars would be enough currency to buy the dress off the Websters and to come back to Cape Cod at least twice. It might even be enough to get her brothers and the boys at school to stop bullying her, and maybe have Rose come live back at home for a while. She walked back with a handful of white shells.

Rose tucked them into her tote. "Are you ready to go home?"

Viviane thought about it for a second, then rushed to get an extra sand dollar for Mathilda. The ground beneath them changed from sand, to gravel, to pavement, and soon they were in the car, driving back home.

In the backseat, Viviane felt the weight of a long day. Before falling asleep, she caught a glimpse of her sister's eyes looking at her in the rear view mirror. Like her smile, they looked light and heavy at the same time.

"Rose, do you think I'll be able to keep the Websters' dress?"

Rose smiled. "Sure, love. I'm sure you will. Get some rest now."

Viviane closed her eyes, and the rattling of the car put her to sleep.

Sometime in her thirties, Viviane saw Race Point Lighthouse again as she was passing a storefront display window in New York City. She stared at the miniature model, varnished and seamless, before noticing her own reflection in the glass. She thought that she looked tired, that she looked juvenile and aged at the same time. There was no fine dividing line between the woman she was and the girl she used to be. She touched the window between her and the replica.

The memory of that afternoon on the beach returned and, with it, what it felt like to be a little girl collecting sand dollars on the beach. It had been over twenty years since Rose killed herself. Signs appeared whenever the anniversary approached—a friend's bathroom vanity showcasing a glass bowl filled with sand dollars, a particular hotel marquee, the smell of the ocean's brine, the squawk of a large seagull—and suddenly she found herself inhabiting that day. The memory wasn't always the same. It shifted, parts of the memory previously hidden were unlocked after a conversation with Cliff or Joy or the twins. Other times she assigned new meaning to a part of the day that had previously meant nothing. This happened the more she learned about Rose, about Joy, about herself. Other times, the memory disappeared entirely, as it had for much of her adult life, and with it a part of herself also disappeared. The more she learned of that day and of Rose, the more it felt like something had been, and always would be hidden from her.

As a teenager, Viviane was overcome by the sense that everyone else was in on a secret she didn't know. She pictured a locked room somewhere in the hills with bolted doors, everyone inside laughing and drinking wine by a stone hearth, knowing everything there was to know.

Then, she felt like there was something she was supposed to remember, but couldn't quite recall. It always felt just out of reach.

Viviane stood staring at the replica lighthouse until someone bumped into her and told her to watch it. She nearly spilled her coffee. There was a nearby park with a fountain, so Viviane walked over and sat on a bench for a while, observing the fountain and finishing her coffee.

She took her phone out from her purse and dialled Cliff's number, but then thought better of it and put the phone back in her bag. She did this a few more times. She finally called her grandmother. When Joy picked up, she hung up and turned off her phone. The anniversary was still a few days away. She'd wait until then to call them all—Uncle Cliff, the twins.

They'd waited a few years to tell her everything, until they thought she was old enough to handle it. Waiting had the opposite effect than they had intended. Everything unravelled, and it had taken Viviane most of her life to put it back together.

A middle-aged woman holding a little girl's hand walked by Viviane. The woman slid her round-toe wedge sandals off her feet, balanced them on the marble edge, then lifted the hem of her red and white polka dot dress. Once she was standing in the fountain, she let it fall, then picked the girl up from beneath her arms. The girl was young, afraid of getting wet, and drew her legs up to her chest. The woman coaxed the young girl into letting them fall, soothed her with secrets whispered into her ear. Viviane assumed the woman was this little girl's mother, and she watched her spin her in circles, the girl's feet skimming the surface, drops of water splashing her shins. They both laughed harder the more they spun.

Rose had given Viviane that day. She had let her in on the secret, she had shown her how they could have been together, if only. It was the closest Viviane had ever felt to being handed the key to that imagined room. It was the last thing Rose did for her.

Viviane sat on the bench, wondering when she had gotten so old. She finished her coffee and for a moment, thought that she might sneeze. There was a feeling that she had come to know, like maybe it would never stop.

Ulcers, Singing

> "I had the idea that the world's so full of pain,
> it must sometimes make a kind of singing.
> And that sequence helps, as much as order helps—
> First an ego, and then pain, and then the singing."
>
> –Robert Hass

1. *First an ego*

SINCE 9 A.M, THE ALARM on my phone had been going off every nine minutes. It was 9:45 a.m. "*Sal!*" I woke up to my roommate banging on my bedroom door.

I untangled myself from the sheets and swung my legs over the side of the bed. I had an appointment at 10:30 a.m and it would take me half an hour to get there. I lay back down for another minute. The days had begun to feel like circuitry—electric and circular. The slew of nurses, general physicians, and gastroenterologists warned that the onset of a chronic illness typically triggered depression, but a diagnosis brought on newfound energy. Apart from the livewire running through my intestines and the existential shock, I still felt lethargic all the time.

In the bathroom mirror, the reflection staring back reminded me of some lines by a prized Montreal poet, Quincy Reeves Hilton, as it often did. My toothbrush stood among a sea of pill bottles. The electric head whirred, straining to clean plaque from my teeth and tossing pellets of spit onto the mirror. I'd recite the lines while brushing, the words progressively unintelligible as my mouth filled with toothpaste, clearing once more every time I spat:

> "I am electric orange hair, unkempt, untidy on
> this blossomed head that aches and pains
> from lack of water." Spit. "My teeth stained red,
> tongue coarse, for I sit and sip this wine,
> a day is a day is a day." Spit. "Widow's peak, emerging,
> I, emerging. Glasses like my grandfather's,
> large and round; head like my father's,
> large and round; teeth like my mother's,
> a necklace of rubbing pearls." Spit. "I am rubbing,
> friction beneath both eyes. Behind spectacles,
> I watch this charade pass me by,
> all smiles and laughter, tears in both eyes."

I rinsed, gurgled, spat, and winked at the man winking back at me, both our breath smelling like gin. *Still drunk,* we thought. Birds chirped outside. They were sober.

My roommate, Trent "Gap-tooth" Weston, was waiting for me outside the bathroom in the narrow hallway leading to our front door. "I made you some scrambled eggs. I started cooking them when I heard your alarm go off. They're cold now." He stood with crossed arms and didn't move when I brushed past him. "I'll leave them in the pan."

"Alright." I coiled my scarf around my neck. "Thanks."

Shutting the door behind me, I heard Trent through the Mayflower glass pane. "*Don't be loud when you come in tonight.*" The frozen wrought-iron banister cooled my hand through my leather glove, but descending a flight of outdoor stairs during a Montreal winter without holding a railing was a suicide mission. I funnelled toward Notre-Dame Street, passing by the red-bricked industrial buildings of Saint-Henri, all of them the same, the same, but different.

It had been three months since my diagnosis, though it felt more like three weeks. The first few days had felt clearer, like a fog had lifted. Every event was imbued with more meaning. The ulcers themselves were benign but rampant, and if we couldn't manage them through medication, they would likely become malignant and lead to something more sinister. The debilitating symptoms and a vague threat of death by cancer loomed over my head, disrupting my days. I bought my groceries and knew better than the rest of those aisle-browsing losers *how* I would die. They sniffed fruit rinds and lifted those dead stuffed birds into their carts without any idea how they too would be stuffed. I pushed my cart with its one loose wheel and knew more about my inevitable stuffing. I was better for it. I had something to point at. The novelty soon wore off. Turkeys looked like turkeys. The days bled into each other.

I took the metro to appointments and sometimes to my university classes, the carts slinking through the underbelly of the city, gusts of wind passing through. When I got to the second floor of the Jewish General Hospital's C-wing, I checked in with the same receptionist who never recognized me. She was either middle aged or very tired. I wondered if she recognized anyone. I sat and waited for her to call my name. In the waiting room there were posters, and one read "Psychological Stages of Chronic Illness & Strategies to Help You Cope." I looked around the room. There was no one else. It must have been for me.

Stage 1: Denial.
Stage 2: Anger.
Stage 3: Bargaining…

Good God, Why? Why me?! Couldn't it be anyone else? What about Trent, or even Quincy? I'd do anything, anything at all! Anything! Oh…Really? My Netflix password? Do you have a pen…

Stage 4: Depression…

I was missing class with guaranteed doctor's notes and

in certain cases was exempt from writing assignments. If anyone was depressed, it was my professors.

Stage 5: Acceptance.

An antiquated five-step process for mourning the death of a loved one, not meant for my life. They were due for an update, though I didn't know what that looked like. Maybe I'd soon advise them. The radiator gurgled up spit and coughed into the clean air. I looked around the room and there was still no one there, so I leaned back and closed my eyes, a wide grin on my face.

II. *...and then pain...*

A few weeks later, I stood on the corner of my street carrying the few possessions I owned in a cardboard box. Trent had kicked me out and given me a couple of days to leave. I had been drinking too much, coming in late at night and waking him up when I did, leaving takeout boxes beside the garbage can. The final straw was when I mistook his bedroom for my own and got into bed with him. His name was on the lease. Mine wasn't. I balanced the box on top of my one suitcase and pulled my phone out from my pocket.

"*Sal,* sweetheart! Where have you been?" my mother's voice rose from the other end. "Your father and I have been trying to reach you."

"Hi, Mom. I've been busy."

"Oh, well, of course you have! It's just so good to talk with you. Your father's in the other room, give me a second and I'll pass him to you."

"I don't have long, Mom. I'll call him later."

"Is everything alright?"

"Yeah. I just wanted to let you know I'll be staying at a friend's place for a little while." I hadn't a clue where I would stay, but going home would be another step backward. I didn't even know exactly why I called her. "I got into a fight with Trent."

"A fight?! How is Trent? We haven't seen him in ages."

"He's charming, Mom. Anyway, if you were thinking of stopping by, for whatever reason, I won't be there."

"Okay, but you'll be going back soon?"

"Sure, Mom."

"Where are you going? Who with?"

"A friend from university. I'll let you know when I get there."

"Okay, Sal. You sure you're fine?"

"I've got to go. Bye, Mom."

She began rattling off suggestions for how I could mend things with Trent to prolong the goodbye. I thought I might finally tell her about the diagnosis but clicked the end call button on the screen, then started looking through my contacts for someone to call before my hands froze.

I was sent to get a blood test on the fifth floor of the E-wing and passed through long narrow corridors until I boarded an elevator. Since my diagnosis, it felt like I was always inside a tunnel or a corridor. My insides were outside, everything a digestive tract we were all passing through.

Inside the elevator, an Orthodox Jewish man wearing slippers asked me what floor. "Fifth," I said, trying not to look at his feet. I nodded as he tipped his hat and pressed the fifth floor. On the ride up, he peeled a banana and took small bites, mashing them audibly against his palate. The elevator creaked open on the fourth floor and he left. Alone, I looked at my own feet, neither of them in slippers, and wondered if the man's pair was hospital-issued, or if he had brought them. On the fifth floor I was given a ticket stub like the ones at my deli, except now I was waiting for a blood test instead of sausages.

Seven patients away from being called to the counter, a nun walked into the waiting room. I looked at her feet, wondered what kind of shoes nuns wear, what sounds they make as they cross through hollow halls, if it sounded like music reverberating through organ pipes. It was strange to think that nuns might be patients too. Hospitals might be the only place you could witness black robes among white lab coats. She took a seat near me.

A small screen with red digits blinked: N-654.

"I'm here for a blood test," I said while approaching the counter.

"Your papers, please."

"Here they are. Dr. Paroli from the Gastroenterology department sent me."

"Your hospital card, *please.*"

I pulled my wallet from my back pocket and nearly spilled all my cards onto the floor. I scrambled for the right card and felt her gaze on the crown of my head.

In the second waiting room, a man with large earlobes sat waiting, his sweater vest holding his gut above his belt buckle, his cowboy hat restraining the beads of sweat from trickling down his forehead. "What will you do, you know?" He spoke to himself, or anyone in the room willing to listen, but spoke with a smile either way. He looked up at the monitor flashing red numbers above the sea of heads. He looked at his ticket stub. "They make you wait all day to send ya' to another waiting room." He chuckled to himself and began to cough, covering his mouth with his fist. He looked up at me after his fit was over. I smiled back at him, but found that his eyes were sad. I looked up at the wide brim just above them before looking away.

N-654. Blink, blink, blink.

I scrambled over to the next room, worried they might skip over my number. When I sat down, they placed my arm in a foam mould, tied a rubber tourniquet around my bicep and stuck a needle in my arm. "You haven't eaten in the past twelve hours, have you?" I looked away as they milked the blood from my arm. "No, ma'am." She filled three syringes with the red syrup.

"You're good to go, honey. Have a nice day."

We were to meet on the corner of Maisonneuve and Saint Mathieu at 2:30 for lunch, as we did every other week. I had forgotten about our lunch until she answered the phone this morning, and then I pretended that's why I had called. I paced around the drug store. Strapped to my wrist, my watch followed as I reached into my pocket to warn Sylvia I'd be late.

Been waiting at the Pharmaprix longer than expected. Sorry. Before sending it, I added, *They even gave me a waiting buzzer.*

I put my phone down. An elderly man rested his cane against a wall and prepared for a self-administered blood pressure test. He removed his brown corduroy jacket, much too light for this weather, and draped it over the stool before sitting. He unbuttoned a cufflink and rolled his right sleeve above his bicep, exposing pale skin and branches of veins. I reached for my own arm, watching the inflatable ring constrict his arm and pull at the loose skin around his tricep. My cell phone buzzed on my lap. The older man whispered, "*Guess not,*" then slowly rose to leave with his corduroy jacket draped over his shoulders.

Don't be sorry. I'll get us a table.

I tried writing something witty but before I could respond, the buzzer shivered across the surface of the table beside me. At the counter, the kind-eyed lady in the white lab coat invited me over with an artificial smile and passed me my medication after an embarrassingly loud explanation of how to administer suppositories. I looked around to make sure nobody had heard. A warm prickle rose from my neck as I quietly thanked her once more.

It was precisely 2:40. I rushed from the drugstore, hoping to avoid running into anybody I knew. The sliding doors released a fog of warm air into the streets, exiling me with a violent gust.

After a few blocks I found the entrance to the Vietnamese restaurant. Sylvia was already sitting at our table, the back of her head to the door. Her hair was cut much shorter.

"*Finally*." She turned at the touch of her shoulder. "Can we please skip the chit chat and go straight to ordering? I haven't eaten all day. You look like you could eat, too."

"Yeah, I've lost some weight."

"How much? What have you been doing? Please tell me your secret. Look at that jawline and those gaunt cheeks." She always kept things light, but her crumpled brow betrayed her concern.

The waiter—who also worked the cash—brought menus to our table, but we ordered without consulting. Number six and eight: rare beef and tripe pho, rare beef and steak flank pho. Sylvia ordered a Vietnamese coffee.

As the waiter left, we turned back to face each other, both smiling. I started talking about the Pharmaprix, how it's a weird undecided place, aisles of food and beauty products in the front, a doctor's office tucked away in the back with shelves of drugs and its own waiting room.

It was precisely 2:55 when our orders arrived. She opened her mouth and began to say something, but I inadvertently cut her off.

"I'm sorry," I said. "You go."

"Alright." She blew on the noodles hanging from her chopsticks. "What's with the suitcase? I knew there was something off."

"How so?"

"Your aura. It's usually white, which is receptive. I had a sense that it was off when you called, but seeing you now, I know for sure."

"So, what is it now?"

She looked around me, then focused on the spot beside my temples.

"Pink."

A party of seven and a cool breeze entered through the sliding wooden doors, the orchids on the windowsills sent to shiver.

"Right, well I don't want you to worry or anything. It's nothing to be concerned about." I glanced downward as she looked up.

The waiter approached our table. "Everything alright?"

"We're fine," we said. I looked back down into the broth after he walked away. "I found out that I have an autoimmune disease. Ulcerative colitis. Essentially, I have ulcers growing in my large intestine."

"Is it dangerous?"

"No. Well, yes, it can be, if untreated. It can lead to internal bleeding and become cancerous." I hesitated to say the c-word, taking a spoon full of broth into my mouth. "I have to monitor it over the next while and take different drugs, but if they don't ease the inflammation then I may need surgery to have my large intestine removed."

"Sal…"

"Don't be sorry. I'm sorry for dampening the mood."

"Don't say that."

We finished the remainder of our pho mostly in silence, spooning warm broth into our mouths. The waiter brought the payment terminal over to our table and smiled while we paid, as if the whole world was made of people lining up to eat soup. He wasn't wearing a lab coat but his face had a pharmaceutical sheen.

"One more thing." I looked up from the payment terminal.

"Yeah?"

"I like your new hair, and I'm going to need a place to stay for a while."

"That's two things."

"Can you lie on your side for us, Mr. O'Connor?"

I rolled over, worrying the gown with the backslit was over-exposing me.

"Okay, Mr. O'Connor, we're going to administer ketamine now. Is that alright?"

"*Mhmmm.*"

"Alright. And remember, after the procedure, it's important that you stay in your bed for at least thirty minutes, okay?"

"*Mhmmm.*"

"And remember, it's crucial that you pass gas, do you understand?"

I nodded. The doctor patted me on the shoulder without a trace of worry lining his forehead.

"Administering the ketamine," he said into the dimly-lit space.

My gurney quickly expanded and grew several times larger; the three doctors circling around me multiplied and broke off into a crowd of a dozen spectral figures. I fixated on the only screen in the room to stabilize myself. They were screening *Star Wars*, which didn't strike me as odd, and I watched a spaceship soaring through a strange-looking galaxy. It was something like forty minutes later, which only felt like a few minutes, that I realized I had been watching the camera lens on the probe they had inserted into my large colon.

This first procedure was covered by my insurance, and so I could do it at a private clinic. Lying in that soft sliver of a cot, I knew that I wouldn't have it so easy next time at the hospital, that I wouldn't be watching *Star Wars*.

After thirty minutes, I lied to the receptionist, telling him my ride was waiting outside. On my walk home along Décarie Boulevard, head tucked into my hood, chin tucked into my chest, dodging snowflakes and keeping my gaze fastened on the path ahead of me, I got the animal feeling that everybody who passed me was only a shadow.

With the arm that wasn't running cold with IV drips, I held *Exterminator!* by William Burroughs open, flipping pages with the one hand. The infusion clinic swarmed with mosquito nurses in blue gowns, who pierced my skin with their proboscis needles, teeth beaming while telling me I had nice veins. The machines whirred, Entyvio slowly dripped through clear tubes into my forearm, bags of liquid hung from IV poles, and everyone sitting in the same reclining chairs was in their fifties, except the one younger man sitting next to me. His hair bunched on his shoulders and he smiled up at the flickering fluorescent lights, eyes closed and receptive to his very own private cosmic message. It was Tuesday. He opened them and looked over at me.

"I used to shit my pants in class."

Sal, nice to meet you too, I wanted to say. "I'm sorry to hear that."

"No need, I've resolved it now. It's all about diet and holistic living." He spoke with tubes in his arm. "You new?"

"Recently diagnosed, yeah."

He surveyed the room. "Listen to the nutritionists, sure, and do the elimination diet. But more importantly, do you smoke weed?"

"Used to."

"No worries, CBD pills do the trick. We live in a wonderful age, all herbs and spices."

Some nurses fluttered into the room, turning off the machines that were sounding off.

"Are you feeling alright, Sal?" my appointed nurse, Guylaine, asked.

"Sure."

"Take Joey with a grain of salt." She winked at him, then at me.

"Guylaine," he said, "you know that the specialists will all tell you different things. We live in the age of science and yet no one agrees on anything—especially autoimmune diseases. Doctors aren't even trained in nutrition! Did you know that? Really, my doctor told me my nutrition had *nothing* to do with my disease."

"You're not entirely wrong, Joey, but please stop prescribing marijuana to the newcomers."

It was his turn to wink. When Guylaine turned around, he handed me a business card. "If you need alternative medicine, you can reach me here."

"Thanks, I might."

"Also, as a gesture of good will," he added, "some free advice: turmeric smoothies."

"Duly noted."

"Give me a ring sometime. We should hang out."

I nodded and he tilted his head back, assuming his grin, and resuming his close-eyed conversation with the fluorescent lights.

"*What did she say*?!"

I sat across another medical professional, this time a nutritionist.

"That his diet had nothing to do with his condition," I repeated.

"Well, let me assure you, Sal…it *does.* And I'll tell you what, the first thing you should be cutting down on is alcohol. Then we can take the time we need to see what foods might be upsetting you. Have you ever tried an elimination diet?"

"No."

The purpose of it was to identify foods that might be aggravating my colon. She explained that for three weeks I would have to avoid nuts, corn, soy, dairy, citrus fruits, nightshade vegetables, wheat, gluten, pork, red meat, eggs, and seafood. I tried to deduce what that left me with.

"Then you reintroduce one food type at a time, for a week, and see if it causes any irritation. You'll keep doing this until you identify foods that cause discomfort. I'd suggest trying cruciferous vegetables with tough stalks first, and then perhaps finer grains that might get stuck in the folds of your mucosa."

"And what can I eat?" I thought I'd take the guesswork out of it.

"Drink water and caffeine-free herbal tea. For food, try to stick to most fruits excluding citrus, most vegetables excluding nightshades, rice, coldwater fish, chicken, and turkey."

I thanked her and left her office, thinking about those stuffed turkeys I had imagined. Standing outside of the office building, waiting for another Uber to pick me up from some distant clinic, I didn't find it so funny anymore.

I met Beatrice in a support group for people living with Crohn's or colitis. There were online weekly meetings organized by Crohn's and Colitis Canada, which I had read about in a pamphlet given to me by a nurse. After attending a few, I learned that a subset of the attendees in the Greater Montreal Region had decided to organize an in-person meeting independent of the organization. One of the organizers, Liu Tai Ling, offered the basement of her parents' restaurant in Chinatown.

Beatrice approached me after the group meeting for a drink. I told her I'd mostly stopped since the diagnosis, but she said that we needed to find respite where we could and that everything in moderation was alright. I hadn't been seeing any of my friends for a while, and her attention felt good. We made a ritual of going for a glass of Merlot at a nearby wine bar on Saint-Laurent Boulevard after meetings, and after a few times, the ritual extended to going back to hers. She had a penthouse condo in the Old Port that looked out over cobblestone streets.

The first time we got naked was the first time I saw a colostomy bag. She explained how it worked, and after a few nights at hers she eventually showed me her stoma, which looked like a distended anus protruding from a hole surgically cut into her abdomen. She helped me shed the taboo and shame of my own disease. When I was fourteen I once heard my cousin talking about sleeping with a girl with a colostomy bag, and how he'd said "you have to slay a few dragons to get to the princess." At the time everyone laughed because he was charming, but thinking back to it made me embarrassed and sad. Imagining people talking about Beatrice like that made me clench my fist. I eventually told her that story.

"People are insensitive," she said, "but especially with anything involving the intestines. It makes them feel uncomfortable and they respond in all sorts of ways. It's not personal, and you get used to it. In time, it becomes easier to talk about it."

Beatrice was in her mid-thirties and had been dealing with Crohn's for eight years. She was slim, a product of the disease, but looked very healthy. She had long brown hair and big, understanding eyes. She was a lawyer, and she often told me she thought the stress of her job was what had caused her disease. Nights spent in bed with her were the best part of all that happened.

"Have you been using suppositories?" she asked me one night while she held me in her arms.

"Yes… why?" Up until then I had tried to keep sex and any talk of the disease separate.

"Doesn't it feel good?" She looked at me, her other hand gripping my thigh, slowly moving upward.

"I, uh." I was stunned and didn't know what to say. It had always felt uncomfortable, and I was always too worried it might slip out to notice if I enjoyed it.

She slid the grey bamboo sheet away and tossed it on the floor. She probed me with her finger and asked if I wanted to try it.

"The male G-spot is in the anus. It's the closest thing you'll ever come to feeling a female orgasm."

I agreed, and within a minute lost control. Before I came, I panicked. I was terrified I might become incontinent. She saw the panic in my eyes but smiled and kept stroking. I was overcome by pulsing waves throughout my body. I felt my rectum clench and squeeze her finger, and my orgasm sent shock waves up to the top of my head and the ends of my fingers. I lay paralyzed for minutes afterwards, coming down from the most intense visceral experience I had ever felt.

"With all our symptoms," she said while getting out of bed, "it's important to maintain a bawdy approach to our bodies." She smiled, knowing what she had just given me.

For weeks after, I used my own finger anytime I touched myself.

Growing up, my aunt Ada couldn't eat wheat. She was the vessel through which I learned about foods like rice crackers and cauliflower-dough pizza. I had always felt a little sorry for Ada.

"I promise I won't tell your parents, but you should really bring it up sooner than later," Ada said. "They'll want to know." Now it was her turn to feel sorry for me. She expressed her pixelated concern through Zoom.

"I know, I just need a bit more time."

My laptop was set up in Sylvia's office. I was glad to have some distance from Ada for the call.

"You're looking thin, dear."

"Exactly… you see, it's not all bad."

At my worst, I had lost thirty-five pounds in six weeks. I had since gained fifteen pounds back. On the worst day, I had used the washroom thirty-seven times.

"Well there's me, as you know, then my cousin Jenna had Crohn's. So it's definitely in the family. Just be careful and take care of yourself."

"Thank you, Ada. I appreciate you talking to me

about it all. My doctors want to know if there was anyone else."

"Anytime, dear, and please...tell your mom and dad as soon as you can."

"I will, Ada. Love you." I closed the laptop screen and sat in silence for a while.

I thought about Ada's distended belly whenever she did eat wheat, about the stories she told me one night after drinking too much wine, about all the times she had shat herself while travelling. I was glad she had shared. It made me feel better about the times I had, too.

"How'd it go?"

I swiveled around. Sylvia was standing in the doorway.

"I'm genetically screwed and thinking about shitting myself."

"Just don't do it in my office chair."

We laughed, but she seemed to sense I could use some space.

"Can I make you dinner tonight?" Sylvia asked.

"I'd love that," I said. "Love you, Syls."

Ada had always shown so much restraint at family dinners. Her selections at restaurants were limited in comparison, and I never thought about how little everyone considered her when making decisions on food. It always broke my heart a little that she was never very good at completely hiding her disappointment, that no matter how hard she tried to be a good sport and not mind, it always peeked through.

Sylvia pressed her ear against my stomach, listening to the borborygmus travelling through my gut.

"It sounds like whales." She held her finger to my mouth and closed her eyes. "*Bbbbbouuuuuuaaghhhhhh.*"

She laughed, looking up at me, and I held my hands over my face.

"Oh, come on, you're lucky, you have marine life living in your belly. Listen: *Eeeerrrrraaaaaaagggghhh.*"

I pretended not to be embarrassed and instead joined in. "*Grrrrrouuuuuuuuahhhhh.*"

We were lying down on the bed in her guest bedroom, staring at the ceiling in the faint dark of the room. Shadows from streetlights crept across the ceiling, painting branches of veins across the walls. We sprawled atop the comforter.

"Alright, Whale Boy, do you have everything you need?"

"I'm good."

"Good." She kissed me on the cheek, and got up to go to her room. "Goodnight."

"*Grrrrrouuuuuuuuahhhhh,*" I said.

"*Bbbbbouuuuuuahhhhhh.*"

I knew I'd never be able to fully repay her. That I had come to love her for what she was doing for me. If I thought about it for too long I'd cry, and I thought it was even sadder that she might see me differently now, like I was weaker or broken. She closed the bedroom door behind her, cutting out any light from the hallway. I turned the lamp on and probed my belly button in the semi-dark room, feeling for my throbbing intestines, hoping to dig out the disease. Sylvia coughed in the next room over.

The worst part was the uncertainty. After excavating my belly button, I got under the sheets and closed my eyes, knowing that I would be awakened in a few hours with a feverish panic and need to use the washroom. I didn't know what might yet come, and there wasn't much else I could do. I had to wait at the station and see what would arrive.

III. "*...and then the singing.*"

Elderly men and women in wheelchairs rolled past me on each side, relatives pushing them from behind. Blankets were folded on their laps and their cheeks looked like they had been hollowed out with spoons. After they passed, there was only the echo of my footsteps. Notes in a long, empty corridor.

The paper crinkled when I sat on Dr. Paroli's examination table. She looked at the wall and poked her fingers into my abdomen, probing for inflammation and maybe also trying to dig it out, the cold latex glove making me tense.

"Good news is we've got you back into remission, which is what we call a stable condition." She rolled my shirt back down and beckoned me toward a chair across from her own. "The bad news is that, as a chronic illness, it can fluctuate throughout your life. Patients tend to go through flare-ups. We don't exactly know why. It could be stress-induced, genetics..."

I was taking notes, looking up to nod and affirm that I was understanding, occasionally omitting a word or two while racing to keep up.

"More good news is that the internal bleeding has stopped. Your calprotectin levels are back to normal, the ulcers are under control, and there will be no need to conduct a colectomy."

The word "conduct" sounded funny, a room of surgeons holding conductor's batons.

"And..." I began, hesitant to reveal myself as a hypochondriac in front of a specialist. "Cancer?"

"For now, it's not a concern, so long as we maintain low inflammation levels."

I nodded, jotting it down.

"Now the neutral news. We'll do everything to keep you in good health, Sal, but a part of chronic illness is learning to live with it. The nurses gave you a pamphlet?"

I nodded, pen down. "Yes, I've seen the poster in your waiting room."

"Good. Of course, with the social aid program accompanying your new medicine, you will always be able to ask questions to their support line. For now, we'll get you to take a blood test to monitor the Entyvio levels in your system and we'll check in again in a few weeks. Alright, Sal?"

I nodded, closing my notebook. I tried to smile but knew I would cry if I let any emotion peek through, no matter how dim.

I looked at all the sullen faces on the metro ride back. A mother sat beside a wheel-locked stroller, her baby wailing from beneath a blanket. The metro car shifted side to side on the rails. My shoulder brushed against the hard plastic walls.

The baby's crying made me anxious, so I got off six stations early and started mindlessly walking back to Sylvia's, passing all the storefronts along the boulevard. A red-and-blue neon light spilled the word *Budweiser* onto the sidewalk. I looked across the street and saw another woman pushing her child in a stroller, and I wondered when it would be the other way around, the kid pushing their mom in a wheelchair. Looking down at my hands, I noticed that they were still quite pale. There wasn't too much pain when I lifted my arm above my head. Today was a good day, I didn't always get off that easy. I thought I would celebrate.

A bell rang above my head when I walked into the bar and knocked the snow off the bottoms of my boots. At the bar there was only one man, with tanned hands and wearing a white wool sweater. I pulled a stool up to the other side of the bar, and a bartender came from a room out back; another waiting room, I thought. Without a class, I was in no rush. I had all day to kill. After ordering,

I put my green notebook on the counter and looked over at the man while the bartender drew my pint.

"*Voila.*"

"*Merci.*" I raised my glass.

"If you need anything, you know where to find me."

She picked a book up from the cash register and began reading. I leaned over and tried to read the title but couldn't catch a good glimpse of it. My phone rang. It was my mother. I ignored the call; there would be time to speak later, to explain. I could picture it: I would go home, hand them the pamphlet, explain what was happening inside me. I took a sip of my beer and listened to the birds chirping outside, and I flipped though my notebook, revisiting my notes to remember everything Dr. Paroli had said. I was moved to write a poem about the birds and the ulcers. Maybe I'd become the next Quincy Reeves Hilton, and someone living with chronic illness would repeat my lines to their reflection in the mirror

The tanned man was one stool closer to mine.

"Whatcha' writing there?" If the accent didn't out him as Eastern Canadian, his openness to strangers did.

I closed my notebook and put the pencil down before sipping what was left of my beer. "A story about ulcers taking over Montreal, then Canada."

The man remained silent, then let out a smoker's cough of a laugh. "If only!" He slapped the counter to accom-pany his hearty laugh. When the bartender asked if I wanted another beer, he signalled for two more, then pointed his thumb at his chest.

"What's your name?"

"Sal O'Connor."

"Gus MacDonald. Good to meet ya."

"Thanks for the beer."

With nothing else to do, we got to talking for a while. He was a fisherman visiting from Petty Harbour–Maddox Cove, a coastal town in Newfoundland. His father had been a fisherman, and his father before him. They had used the same fishing trawler all that time and Gus had lived his whole life in the same timberclad shack he was born in. This was his first time in Montreal. He could remember his old man talking about the good days spent drinking in Montreal, but I was sure Gus had picked the wrong season to visit.

"And what is it you do, Sal?"

"I'm not too sure anymore. I'm a student between classes, let's say."

"I can understand that. I'm a man between catches. Mind if I sit closer?" he asked, already approaching.

He talked about his boat, about the large trawler nets that dragged across the bottom of the ocean and the different fish he caught, about how hard it was for him to find a reliable deckhand since he didn't have any progeny. It was a nice idea to get so far away from home, to live on a boat elsewhere for a while. I took his information knowing I would never follow up, but it was nice to fantasize.

"It'll be eight dollars for your first," the bartender

said. I settled my tab and soon the bell rang above my head once more, as I waved to Gus over my shoulder and hoped I'd see him again.

The air cut against my face and sobered me up a bit as I stepped outside, but I was still drunk. I stood on the sidewalk and looked in both directions. The westerly wind blew eastward; I tucked my chin into my scarf.

On my way back to Sylvia's, I began to better recognize my surroundings. Trent's wasn't too far. I decided I would stop by to try and smooth things over, try and make it ours again. I missed him. This time I'd make my own eggs, wake at the first alarm, sign the lease. I would cut down on my drinking. I would change my habits, learn to live with it. In some ways, I owed him. He was the one that found me in bed clutching at my stomach and drove me to the ER. We had meant to go to the market on a Sunday, and when he came into my bedroom at noon the curtains were drawn and I was curled like an overcooked shrimp—which I could still eat. I'd always be grateful to him, despite what happened.

I texted Sylvia, asking if I could make her dinner that night. She texted back, "*Bbbbbouuuuuahhhhhh.*"

I passed a tall office building I had seen before. It might have been the beers, or the new medication, or a compound of both, but I pictured each floor occupied with ulcers wearing suits, sitting at desks, answering phone calls, and filling out Excel sheets. Two ulcers laughed by the water cooler, and I couldn't help but laugh with them. A woman pushing a carriage with a pink baby ulcer strolled past me, and both of them waved. While walking past the cedars lining the perimeter of the corporate parking lot, I heard a nest of birds chirping from within their branches, repeating the same pattern of notes.

The notes played over in my head sounding like a song I knew even after the cedars were far behind. *Coo-ah-coo-coo-coo.* I tried to figure out the song but couldn't place it, and instead guessed the type of bird, which I also recognized. I got to thinking that there was a whole symphony of Mourning Doves in that bush, and it made me grin. I liked to think there were a thousand birds living in that one nest, squatting in the cedars and hiding from the passing pedestrians and streaming traffic.

The world felt like it had lifted and I was struck with the sensation that I could go on walking forever into the lightness of it all, that it could all burn down and would be built up again if it did. I held on to the feeling and let it sit for a while, backdropped by the sounds of my footsteps, and the birds chirping from within their nest. This feeling sustained itself until the side streets led to a boulevard, and the quietness of the borough was disrupted by the traffic; but even the traffic sounded softer.

Winter would turn to spring, turn to summer, turn to fall, back to winter, then the leaves would be gone and the birds would still be singing and I might call my parents. On the Atlantic Ocean, a small fishing boat could take me elsewhere. In Montreal, I could get a job working with my ulcers. I closed my eyes. I forgot the cold weather around me, smelled the salt carried on the Atlantic winds. There were ulcers living in the city, but there was also a sailboat, other cities, fathoms of ocean, and there were Mourning Doves. I was drunk; the birds, they were sober, and they were all of them singing.

Chicken in Two Parts

"TOMMOROW I'M PULLING my eyes out, Seymour."

Tweedy threw a rock at the side of the passenger train, and it flew out into the night. We watched it soar through the dark sky by the light of the train windows, and then it disappeared, like all the faces in the rows of those seats.

"We could gouge them out," I said. "My grandma's got a collection of antique spoons."

I picked up a pebble and repeated the same motion: a clink of metal, a spark, then a siffling through the air.

Tweedy and I were drinking beers in a shallow ditch by the tracks tucked behind a field of barley, as we did every summer weekend. Last weekend he stood on the tracks to see if he could outlast the oncoming train after depleting a pocketful of pebbles and a flask of Kraken Rum. I watched in horror and admiration—his face growing brighter in the headlights, his smile growing wider—as I wondered what fuelled the quiet man standing on those rails.

At the last second, Tweedy dove into a bush with poison ivy. His eyes were now swollen half-shut.

"We should've gotten you to a hospital," I said. "You look terrible."

We watched the train take the bend. Its tail curved with the tracks, the whole of it escaping beyond these fields, all those people on board further along to wherever they had to go. The night smelled of chimney smoke and fires burning in the yards of nearby barns. I thought about how no one here ever really had anywhere to go. My summers spent in the country with Grandma slowed the other nine months in Montreal with my parents; each summer, the same stop, the same station. Then, at the end of it, I stuffed my clothes into a suitcase and boarded again.

My mother grew up on her parents' farm just outside of Sackville, New Brunswick, and my father grew up in Montreal. When Mom found out she was pregnant, they decided they wanted me to experience both worlds. My childhood summers were spent in New Brunswick, wreaking havoc on neighbouring farms with Tweedy, while the school months were spent in Montreal. When I turned twelve or thirteen I didn't want to spend my summers there anymore, but my parents insisted, and when Grandpa passed away there was plenty of work to be done around the farm, so I kept coming around to help Grandma out. It was nice to reconnect with Tweedy, who had never lived anywhere outside of Sackville and wasn't the type to stay in touch by text or take a train into Montreal.

Another engine sounded somewhere farther off, and Tweedy looked at me like I knew what to do. The fields of barley leaned in. Tweedy popped the collar on his favourite hand-me-down tweed jacket—his namesake.

"Your turn," he said.

I took a moment to process what he was saying. "You can't be serious."

"I made it out, didn't I?"

"Barely," I said, looking at his eyes.

He studied the ground and picked up the perfect rock; then, before I understood what he was doing, hurled it at my face. I ducked before it could hit me in the forehead.

"*What the fuck's wrong with you*?"

"You spend too much time with your grandma, that's what's wrong with *you*," Tweedy replied. "You should hang out with me more. I can teach you some things."

I rubbed the ghosted spot on my face where the rock almost hit me. "How would I explain two black eyes and a boulder-sized bump on my forehead to my parents?"

"People fall. Your loss though. Now you'll be returning home without a story to tell, without a lesson learned." Tweedy liked to speak in mystical terms, like he had some Taoist lessons to impart.

The train was approaching, the sound of its engine growing in momentum. My temples were pulsing, whole head throbbing.

"Since when was drinking and tossing rocks not enough?"

"Suit yourself, city boy." Tweedy took his flat cap off and dropped it on the ground. He limped toward the rails and I felt a pang of guilt. Tweedy was tall, probably six foot three or something, at least a head taller than me, and lanky. He looked like a stick. One of his legs was slightly shorter than the other, so he walked with a minor limp. He had scraggy, curly hair, and when his eyes weren't nearly swollen shut, they were big, blue, and bulging. I couldn't watch him hurt himself anymore. He already needed to be hospitalized.

"*Wait*," I called after him. "Fine, I'll do it." He spun on his heels, a grin already forming on his face. "You're like a chicken with its head cut off," I added.

I finished my beer and made my way to the tracks. It was getting late. I thought about my grandma and hoped that she had already gone to bed, but she was likely sitting on the front porch in the moonlight, listening to show tunes on the radio and waiting for me to get home.

"And the show begins." Tweedy winked at me, though his eyes were already halfway there. I gave him the finger and he began singing "Hello! Ma Baby" in the style of Michigan J. Frog from *The Bugs Bunny Show*, kicking his legs out and tipping his flat cap.

The rails drummed beneath my boots and my legs shook. I tried to fight it off. I didn't want Tweedy thinking that the city had made me soft. The lights grew brighter, the train ticking on, the conductor growing clearer. I saw the panic-stricken look on his face. Tweedy stood there with a shit-eating grin, still kicking his legs out, holding his thumb up as if he were trying to catch a ride. I was standing both in front of the train and in front of Tweedy. He pointed to a bushy spot without poison ivy beside the rails.

I didn't feel a layer of leaves if there was one. If there was, it dissolved as soon as my body tore through it. I crashed into branches and landed on gravel while a thundering noise whizzed past me. It grew lighter before it grew dark again. I lay still, taking inventory of all my limbs, waiting for a wave of pain to surge through my body. I rolled onto my back and looked up at the lucky stars—all of them winking, only one flashing across the sky before dissolving. I didn't rush to get up. Instead, I rested on the gravel while Tweedy danced around the tracks, howling at the moon.

"That's gotta be a game-of-chicken world record! *Awwoooooo!* The student becomes the sensei."

Lying there, I couldn't help but smile. We used to jump in cold lakes together—our clothes bunched in a pile by some bushes—then run home to Grandma if any leeches stuck to our legs. We tipped cows at the age of twelve; four years later we escalated to shearing crop circles, encrypting alien messages into corn fields for the news reporters to decipher. These were the same idle days spent eating pumpernickel crust and turkey sandwiches in the shade of trees, bowered in supine positions. I thought then that we would do these sorts of things every day for the rest of our lives.

Now, I felt like an outsider when I visited. My relationship with Tweedy was like that of a local and a tourist. I wanted to tell myself that it was symbiotic, that he was getting something out of seeing me and catching up too, but I couldn't shake this feeling that I was visiting occasionally for my own voyeuristic benefit, that I was keeping a distance between us, and that distance was at his expense and my benefit. I thought he needed help, but I wasn't doing anything about it. I liked that our relationship gave me something that I didn't get with my friends in Montreal. I liked to come back and occasionally benefit from the reckless nature of his self-destructive tendencies, the ones we used to share. I had moved on and he hadn't, and I told myself there was nothing I could really do to change Tweedy. He was the way he was, and only he could help himself. I wasn't sure I believed it. Now, I only wanted to get back home.

Tweedy pulled me up by the arm and patted me on the back. "Now there's a story you can take to Montreal."

He held me just above the elbow and helped me limp toward my bike.

"They wouldn't believe me. They lack imagination for anything outside the city."

"But *us,*" he said, looking over the fields and up at the moon, "we have what we need out here."

I put my arm around his shoulders and let him carry my weight.

"Same time next weekend?" Tweedy asked.

"I can't, my grandma's having her siblings over for the weekend and I'm helping play host. You know the script: put something nice on, slick my hair back, smile and wave, refill the drinks. The regular shit." Tweedy jumped out of the ditch then turned back, extending his arm to help me out. "She likes to parade me around every summer."

"Pearl and Glenn? And what am I supposed to do?" he asked.

"And Shannon and Bob...and I don't know." I shrugged. "Figure something out."

"You're going to make me spend the evenings with my dad?"

"I'll try to visit you at the gas station before dinner."

"Well, I guess the weekend after then," he offered.

"I'll text you. I've got some work for my online summer courses that I'm trying to catch up on. I'm already falling behind with all the help Grandma needs around the farm."

"You're going back home soon, aren't you?"

I swung my leg over my bike and cradled the seat beneath my crotch.

"Yeah."

"You'll catch up then."

"It's not that simple," I said.

Tweedy sighed and nodded his head. "It always is."

I grabbed the handlebars and dug my heels into the pedal-stirrups, pretending to spank its hide. Tweedy waved and turned to walk away.

"Hey, Tweedy—" He turned around to look back at me. "Go see a doctor."

"I'll be fine," he said.

"Alright. Love you, buddy."

"Whatever you say."

I kicked off and peddled home. Swerving along the dirt road, I looked over my shoulder before taking the first bend. Tweedy was still standing in the same spot. I raised my hand but he didn't wave back. I felt a stone in my stomach as his silhouette was lost behind the barley.

For the length of my bike ride home, I peddled standing up. I closed my eyes and listened to the sounds of chickens stirring, my tires kicking up the dirt road; in the moonlight, the fields were nested with cows. Riding my bike through the dirt roads after drinking invoked all the past summers spent at Grandma's farm—it wasn't the wind against my face but time itself, and I was cutting through it. A Belgian Malinois jumped out from a field and began trotting at my heels, looking up at me. It made me think of Odin.

Grandma and Grandpa once had a Belgian Malinois named Odin, with one brown eye and one light blue eye. They trained him to watch over the farm animals. The last summer that my grandpa was alive he showed me how to milk the cows. In the early morning, it wasn't Grandpa who woke me, but the weight of Odin's body on the bed, his sandpaper tongue scraping my forehead before Grandpa's belly breached the doorframe. He patted my feet beneath the duvet, readjusted his suspenders, then left the room. Odin sat beside the foot of the bed, obedient. I put my clothes on, obedient.

One morning during Grandpa's last summer, when I was sixteen, it was my grandpa's hands that shook me from my sleep. I looked up into his eyes. They looked back at me, expressing something I didn't recognize. The bedside lamp was turned on, and beyond the penumbra of the lampshade, the room was dark. There were no clothes laid out and I rushed outside in my pajamas. Odin had gotten into the pigsty overnight and attacked a pig named Beth. I watched Beth strain to breathe below Grandpa's boot, her belly rising and falling as her eyes looked somewhere further. Grandpa told me to go find him, and I was scared for Odin.

After he pulled the trigger, Grandpa stood above Beth's corpse. He let out a long sigh, then gently cried. I don't think he knew I was watching him from farther off. I learned that when you care about something, sometimes the only thing you can do is show mercy. Before the next summer, Odin was gone and so was Grandpa. I wondered if Grandpa had been shown mercy. Someone told me that his death was a pulled plug and a flatline on a screen. I didn't get the chance to visit him in hospital, but I remember his death through my mother's face. She had just gotten home from the grocery store when she listened to the voicemail.

The Belgian Malinois veered off a few streets before mine. I dropped my bike by the side of the house when I got home. The porch lights were on and my grandma was fast asleep. I kissed her gently on the forehead before waking her up, taking her elbow and helping her out of the chair.

Everyone in town knew Tweedy's dad. He owned the gas station, and either his shirts smelled like petrol or his breath smelled of ethanol.

I rode into the lot and propped my bike onto its kickstand next to Ray's motorbike. The station was off the main road and sat in between a bunch of fields. Tweedy stood behind the counter and waved me in through the shop window, but I was stopped before I could enter.

"Seymour." Ray walked over from the outdoor bathroom, holding a key tied to a large wooden cooking spoon. "What have you idiots been doing? What the fuck happened to Teddy's eyes?" He grumbled, which meant he wasn't drunk. He mumbled when drinking.

"Hi Ray. We've just been down by the tracks. He fell into a bush of poison ivy."

"I see you've corroborated your stories. Good to know you both think I'm an idiot." He bit off a chunk of beef jerky and chewed it with his mouth open. "When are you guys going to do something productive with your time?"

Tweedy got his big, bulging blue eyes from Ray, but Ray's were always red around the rims. He had dry spit at the corners of his lips, and even when he was angry he would grin with one side of his mouth. You never knew what mood he'd be in; I wasn't the only one in town who felt that way.

"We're not causing any trouble. I keep a good eye on Tweedy, sir."

"Don't call him that stupid name. That's the problem with Teddy. He needs someone to look after him and tell him what to do."

Tweedy came out from the shop.

"Teddy, are there any customers inside? You can't just leave the till."

Barring my bike and Ray's motorbike, the parking lot was empty.

"No, Dad. I'm not an idiot. I wouldn't leave the cash unsupervised."

"Don't get clever with me, Teddy. Seymour and I were just talking about your prospects in life… It was a brief conversation."

Tweedy stood there looking at the ground. I never knew what to do when Ray berated Tweedy in front of me. This tendency wasn't reserved exclusively for me. My grandma had commented on it. Sometimes I pushed back and told Ray all the good ideas for businesses Tweedy had pitched to me, but that never seemed to help. He'd just laugh them off and continue his litany of insults. There was of course the gas station, which Tweedy would presumably inherit. Still, Ray found fault in this too: *leech*, *deadbeat waiting for his pops to croak*, *no drive*, etc.

"I hear you're busy tonight, Seymour, so I get the privilege of Teddy's presence on a weekend for once… I can't wait." Ray grinned, shook my hand, and went back into the gas station.

"I'm sorry about tonight, man… I wish I didn't have this dinner."

"Ah, it's alright. My shift is almost over and then I'll probably go to a bar in town. Maybe I'll stop by the tracks for a bit first, clear my head."

He pulled a flask out from the back of his jeans, and tipped it to me. "Want some?"

"I'm good, man. I've got to get going." We hugged and I was off as quick as I had come. When I turned onto the road, I looked back toward the gas station to say one final goodbye, but Tweedy was gone. He must have already gone inside.

Ever since I'd known Tweedy, even when we were younger, Ray had always been rough on him. I'm not sure if it was ever physical. If it was, Tweedy never mentioned it. But it bothered Tweedy enough that I think he found ways to physically hurt himself anyway. As a young boy,

I remember wondering why no one ever stepped in. *It's none of our business*, or, *it's not our place to say.* Over time, without even noticing it, I had adopted the same approach. Biking along, I wished I had said something, knowing still that it would have no effect at all.

When I got home, there was a handwritten note on the kitchen counter.

I'm upstairs getting ready. Guests are coming earlier than expected. Please take care of the chicken. Love, Grandma.

Something adorable about my grandma was that she always signed her notes like a love letter. I rubbed the chicken in oil, stuffed it with fresh seasoning, slid squares of butter beneath the skin, then cracked some pepper over it. Preheating the oven would take too long and I still had to get ready, so I set it to 400 and didn't wait before putting the chicken in.

Upstairs I rushed to get ready, but felt a wave of fatigue. Half-dressed, I lay on my bed and rested my eyes for a couple of minutes.

"Seymour, what's that smell?" my grandma's voice rang from the other room.

"Nothing!" I sprang up from the bed and ran down the stairs while tucking in my shirt, opening the oven door when I got to the kitchen. The rusty hinges unleashed a cloud of billowing smoke from beneath a burned, hollowed carcass. I fanned manically with a ragged dish towel.

"Seymour? What am I smelling?"

"Nothing–" I turned the radio up, hoping the sound might somehow detract from the smell.

"Is something *burning*?" Her footsteps fell against the stairs.

I tried to make myself presentable so that one of us might be pleasing. I patted the pleats in my pants and rushed to the cupboard filled with herbs, shuffling through them to find some sage or thyme.

"What happened?" she asked when she came into the kitchen. "*Seymour,* I put you in charge of the chicken. Didn't you read my note? What will they eat now? What will they think? There's not enough time."

"We can offer them a vegetarian meal?" I shrugged and gave a nervous smile.

"On a farm with chickens, pigs, and cows, we offer our guests potatoes?"

Grandma put on an apron then flipped the chicken over and observed the bottom half. The white apron with yellow stripes fell loose over her frame, and I noticed the loose skin around her neck. I poured her a glass of wine and tied the apron above her waist. A fleeting sadness came over me thinking about how she had aged.

"It's salvageable," she said. There were deep wells beneath her eyes. "It's mainly the skin that's blackened. Would you cut out the pieces that are usable and put them on a plate? We can keep them in the oven."

"Go on and finish upstairs," I told her. "I'll take care of things until they arrive."

She took a moment to smile at me before heading out of the room.

"Oh—" she shouted back from the stairwell. "And would you mash the potatoes and cook down some onions please?"

The landline rang, but before I could reach it, Grandma called down to let me know she had it. She hadn't made the transition to a cell phone despite her children's insistence.

I opened a window and tried to fan the rest of the smoke out. Aunt Shannon and Uncle Bob were asthmatic. Uncle Glenn and Aunt Pearl weren't, but the chicken might do them in if the smoke didn't. They weren't really aunts and uncles, but great aunts and great uncles. They lived a few roads down and visited me every summer.

"Shannon and Bob will be late," she shouted from upstairs.

"Buys us some time," I murmured.

"First they call to say they'll be earlier than usual, so I have to scramble," she carried on. "And then they call to say they'll actually be later than usual. Figures..."

I salvaged what I could from the chicken. The potatoes were mashed, then stirred in with cooking cream, cold butter, green onions, and cream cheese, and I had moved on to cooking down the onions. I turned the radio up and wiped the tears from my eyes. The doorbell finally rang about thirty minutes later.

"I got it!" I passed by the wood panel walls and the

portraits hanging in the hallway and moved into the vestibule, wiping my hands on a towel.

I opened the front door and the acrid smell of old cigarettes entered the house.

"Seymour!"

Aunt Pearl wrapped me in a long embrace. She was a stout woman who could knock me off my heels, but caught me before she did. I was choking on all her hair, inhaling the stench of cigarettes, gladly hoping it might mask the scent of burned chicken. I looked over her shoulder and watched Uncle Glenn lean on his cane and struggle to get his feet over the door frame. He leaned over and picked a chip of red paint from the frame.

"You need to repaint the door, Seymour."

"It's great to see you both, too."

"You look older every year." Aunt Pearl held me at arm's length and took me all in. I became self-conscious.

"I get older every year."

Aunt Pearl's nostrils flared, and she started sniffing the air. "What's that smell?"

"It's just the chicken. It's fine."

"Why'd you paint over the door hinges?" Uncle Glenn was still studying the door. "That's where it's flaking." He peered over his horn-rimmed glasses that would have fallen off his face if it weren't for his large, purple nose.

"I'll give it a new coat, then."

"No, no, no, you need to chip it off."

"I'll chip it off, then. Would you like to come into the living room? Grandma will be down soon."

"That's right!" Aunt Pearl chimed in. "Where's that sister of mine?"

The odour wasn't restricted to her hair, and she had attempted to mask it with a heavy violet perfume. We walked past portraits of former versions of themselves, which neither of them bothered to survey. The floorboards creaked beneath Aunt Pearl.

"She'll be down soon. I need to finish prepping, but can I get either of you a drink?"

"Whiskey for me." Uncle Glenn trailed behind.

"What wines do you have?" They hadn't brought anything with them.

"What do you prefer?"

"A Chardonnay if you have," she said. "Otherwise, anything will do."

I left them behind and walked toward the kitchen.

"Oh, and Seymour—" I turned around on my heels. "You'll tell us all about your parents and the city and your schooling when you get back, won't you?"

"Of course."

"Oh, and what's that boy's name..." She snapped her fingers repeatedly while looking up at the ceiling for it. "That friend of yours?"

"Teddy," I offered.

"*Yes*! Teddy. That's the one. Will he be joining us tonight?"

"Unfortunately not. He's working at the gas station."

"Ah—" She frowned. "That's too bad, that boy could

use some good company and better role models. Oh well!"

I smiled and told them I'd be right back. I sighed once I got into the kitchen. The dish towel hanging from the oven door had small sunflowers printed on it that made me think of an old dress Grandma used to wear. I stood there for a moment, looking at nothing in particular.

I was seven years old when I first watched Grandma kill a chicken. We walked along the path toward the hen house, her gentle white dress with yellow flowers billowing. Inside the chickens welcomed us, flocking at the expectation of seeds. Grandma bent over, swept her arm across the ground and came up with an upturned chicken. The rest of the brood scattered out, and a few feathers landed softly on the wood shavings and straw floor. She held it by the shanks below its bald feet and caught the chicken's head between two fingers. She jerked her wrist and pulled until I heard a hollow pop. Its body quivered. She took my hand and walked me back to the house, the limp chicken hanging from her other hand. Being pulled along, I watched the way her dress fell upon her back, the creases in the fabric, those tiny yellow flowers printed all across it. I remember being confused, and that the chicken dinner that night tasted different.

There was an unopened bottle of Chardonnay in the fridge, alongside a few bottles of beer that I had bought the night before. I poured Aunt Pearl a glass of wine and myself a beer, and thought of Tweedy. I wondered what he might be doing right now. A sharp twinge seized my leg, and I shifted my weight onto my other foot

"*Shit*," I said.

"Are you alright?"

My grandma appeared around the corner, and I was glad to see her.

"Yeah, I'm fine. I'm just going to finish with the onions and then we'll be ready to eat."

"What happened to your leg?"

"Nothing, I think I stepped on it wrong."

She crossed her arms, knowing and disapproving all at once. "You hurt yourself doing something dangerous with Teddy, didn't you?"

"It has nothing to do with Teddy, Grandma."

She didn't budge. "He's a sweet boy, Seymour, and I know you've known him forever. I like him, but just be careful, okay? At least when his mom was still here there was a voice of reason around. I drove by the station and saw him the other day. He looked like death, both his eyes swollen shut."

"I know, Grandma." I handed her the glass of Chardonnay. "Would you bring this to Aunt Pearl?"

"What about the others?"

"Uncle Bob and Aunt Shannon still aren't here yet, and Uncle Glenn wants a whiskey. Would you get him one for me, please?"

"Yes, of course—there aren't enough onions there. Would you cook some more down?"

I nodded.

"Good. Oh, and Seymour?"

I looked up at her.

"Come join us as soon as you're done. They miss you, you know."

She took the glass of Chardonnay from the counter and disappeared into the living room. I turned the volume on the radio up, but it was no longer playing music. A man's voice was recounting the hourly news. I draped the dish towel over my shoulder and began chopping the onions. The room thickened with the smell of acidic vapors and stale crushed skins. I saw a cartoon hand rise out of the cloud of fumes and poke at me, my eyes welling up with tears. Laughter erupted and spilled in from the living room. I wiped my eyes with the back of my hand.

The radio announced that earlier that evening, a boy had been down by the tracks and was struck by a train. My leg seized up. I put the knife down and looked into the pile of onions. The conductor was being interviewed and told the reporter that there was nothing he could have done. He'd pulled the brake, but it was too late. The picture of swaying barley passed through my mind. I imagined a whole field leaning in toward my grandma's farm, listening to the broadcast. Farther, I heard a distant train approaching the house.

For a few moments after the radio announced the death, I thought of my mother's face, and then of

Tweedy. The doorbell rang and Grandma called my name from the other room. A gust of wind blew through the window and bandied the curtains, brought the world in from outside.

Before I answered, or managed to leave the spot where I was standing, I thought of his silhouette standing by the road, about the fields of barley leaning inward. I thought about the passengers on the train. I saw the moonlight reflecting off his face, a white sheet pulled over his eyes. There was no one to blame for this. The conductor had pulled the emergency brakes. I stood above the radio thinking of Odin, the mercy he had been shown, thinking of the chicken we were eating and thinking of Grandpa and of Grandma, thinking of Mom and Dad and Pearl and Glenn and Shannon and Bob. I thought of everyone I ever knew. The news carried on. I hoped he had been shown mercy.

Love Cinema

We were waiting in a line, which wrapped around the corner of Duluth, when I noticed that the trees across the street looked like erections. Of course they didn't, but I was excited, nervous, and thinking of erections. I wore a thrifted Village des Valeurs fur coat and a scarf around my neck. As the wind blew through the trees, the last of the leaves fell to the ground. Goosebumps lined my arms as I looked over at Fanny. Above her, the iconic yellow marquee with red and black letters spelled "Cinéma L'Amour," and behind her there were posters of naked women in the windows. It was sometime in mid-November. The first snowfall of the season coated our shoulders with a thin layer of snowflakes, and crowds of people continued to march past along Saint-Laurent Boulevard.

"Have you ever watched porn with somebody else?" Fanny asked as we inched forward.

"Yeah," I said. "The first time I watched it was on my family desktop with a couple of friends. We promised not to watch each other. I had to stand in the corner of the room."

"Weird. I meant with a girlfriend."

"Oh, yeah," I lied, "I've done that too."

We went quiet again. I had met Fanny in the third class of a graduate creative writing workshop after she'd skipped the first two. When Fanny first walked in, I thought she was a replacement faculty member. She wore a beige peacoat and kept her hair in a bun with two chopsticks, which she later told me were hair sticks. When the instructor arrived, I tapped her on the arm. She turned to me with an unfamiliar expression, as if expecting a good story. It took me by surprise. I began talking. I told her that she had missed everything in the first two classes, that the Big Man upstairs had descended from above, shook everybody's hand, informed us that we would each pen a Giller Prize–winning book. The way she smiled at me looked new.

We started going for drinks after class, and last time she rambled on about a double Abel Ferrara screening that her ex was guest-programming at Cinéma L'Amour. Her ex had been invited to collaborate on curating films because the cinema was trying to appeal to a wider audience. Fanny spoke about the pornographic chic era—something about libertine sensibilities and the grind-houses of 1970s New York City coming to an end—both tipsy and sounding like she was reciting from a script. Ferrara was a relic worth spotlighting, I was told, so she invited me to attend a double screening of *The Driller Killer* (1979) and *9 Lives of a Wet Pussy* (1976). *The Driller Killer* was a black-comedy slasher movie, and *9 Lives of a Wet Pussy,* well... it suited the venue.

In line outside Cinéma L'Amour, things were still awkward between us. I had brought a flask with me, which I was keeping on reserve for the screening. I craned my neck, hoping I'd find something to talk about. The buildings across the street were covered in graffiti, the snow fell at a slant, an alleyway dumpster was brimming with industrial garbage bags, the black plastic turning white where unknown objects strained to pierce through. They may have been filled with hair sticks.

A middle-aged man in a dress shirt greeted us at the counter and asked us for our money, his long hair brushing dandruff on his shoulders. I recognized the older man beside him, grabbing fistfuls of popcorn from a large silver bowl and cramming it into his mouth. He was the owner of the theatre and had been profiled for an online issue of *The Bleak Midwinter.* The article, titled "Cinéma L'Amour: Adult Theatre's Saving Grace," had opened with the line, "Though big-screen porn has long been dwindling from pop-culture, Montreal's Cinéma L'Amour resists through the sheer act of existing, and continues to buck its seemingly inevitable demise." The owner was a Holocaust survivor. When asked to speak about his life in the New World, about why, after all he had seen, he had decided to run an adult cinema, he simply said, "Porn makes money."

"I'll cover it." Fanny's arm extended and her credit card pushed past me, tapping the terminal before I had the chance to pull my wallet out. I awkwardly thanked her and kept walking ahead.

"I couldn't come to this alone. That would be weird," she said. "I need an accomplice."

"That's fine." I wondered if she was using me as a pawn to signal she had moved on from her ex.

"Paying for this is me showing gratitude, Seymour. Don't get used to it."

I harped on it anyway, not sure if this was even a date, which is what I hoped it was.

I followed Fanny past the concession stand and walked into the theatre. We shuffled down the aisle, passing rows of red seats imprinted with the ghosts of lonely old men and bored middle-aged couples. I shuddered under my coat. The lemon-scented air freshener caught in the pockets of fabric got me thinking that we should have at least slept together before coming here. The old walls led up to an ornate ceiling with flaking paint, a horseshoe balcony, and the VIP booths. I imagined something dripping from above.

"They design theatres so that the acoustics are better in the centre of the room," I said.

Fanny looked at me with a blank expression. She surveyed the room, looking for someone else. "Are you here for the acoustics?" she asked.

The room was dark enough to hide that I was blushing. "What would you suggest?"

"Let's pick a corner. I want to observe." We sat down at the back of the theatre, and I ironed out the pleats in my pants, feeling the flask beneath my hand. I pulled it out and dangled it in the air.

Fanny's knee brushed against mine. Fanny Belhomme, who hailed from New York and had French ancestry and pedigree, who had come to Montreal to pursue creative writing, sitting next to an English literature student who had taken one creative writing workshop and who had grown up in the suburbs. "Your first good idea." She grabbed the flask and removed her jacket, flinging it over the seat in front of her.

During her junior year of high school, her father homeschooled her so they could sail the East coast toward the Caribbean. She spent a summer living on her grandmother's farm in Arizona when she was thirteen. She was fourteen when she smoked her first cigarette, after losing her virginity to a guy named Robbie, a friend of her older brother. Whenever she told me these stories, I withheld my life of playing Sandman at the park down my street, of Marco Polo in public pools, of house parties in carpeted basements. Yet despite this, here she was sitting next to me, drinking from my flask.

"I read that people swap partners in the VIP booths upstairs," I said.

"Better hold me tight, then." She laughed, settling into her seat as the previews began. She passed the flask back to me. I took a long, warm swig.

The previews were pornographic. We were getting drunk and made salacious comments. It felt like a barrier was breaking down between us, that all it took was alcohol and some exposed skin. *For what I pay my tutor, I wish that's how I got fucked.* The whole world felt like it was falling into my lap.

The curtains had only parted two thirds of the way for the previews. Now the room went dark and the curtain pulled back to reveal the full screen as *The Driller Killer* began. Red LED lights lit up the aisle. The house lights dimmed. I felt a hand patting at my pockets, searching for the flask. Only after exploring my ribs and thighs did it finally land on the side of my leg. I let the hand have it.

Near the end of the first feature, as the failed artist and anti-hero Reno Miller is power-drilling into a homeless man, Fanny leaned into me. "This programming is brilliant. It highlights the distinct evolution in Ferrara's style within only a three-year period," she whispered. "It's an important one. He left behind his lascivious films and began gearing toward a commercial sensibility. That's important, you know, and to be lamented. The wheels of time and capitalism move on and there's nothing we can do to stop it, and it changes *everything.* Mediums of art, art itself, even porn."

I nodded to acknowledge the significance of this. After *The Driller Killer* we went into the lobby for intermission. Pushed together by the crowd, Fanny's eyes darted across the room while she spoke absently about Abel Ferrara's life in New York City. "Gloria!" Fanny turned from me mid-sentence. "A wonderful showing. What a nice touch using the original analog film."

Gloria, a woman in her early- to mid-thirties with a mauve pixie cut and snake tattoos around her neck, approached and eased her way into our huddle.

"*So* glad you could make it." They kissed cheeks. "Can you believe that it's not the original film? We were worried about it getting caught in the reel, so we screen-captured the original film and had a laptop hooked up to the projector… What you're actually watching is an MP4 file." They both laughed as if this was the most ludicrous thing they had ever heard.

"Gloria, this is Seymour. Seymour, Gloria, my ex."

"Hi, my name's Seymour." I extended a stiff handshake and thought *Idiot, she just said your name.*

"Delightful to meet you, Seymour. What did you think of the screening?"

"It was gory. I'm sure it was incredible in the centre of the theatre. The acoustics are best there." They both looked at me with plastic smiles. The movie was about a serial killer slaughtering people with a drill, and all I could say was *it was gory.* Great, I should consider becoming a critic.

They kept talking and I tried to play it off like I wasn't embarrassed. I signalled I was going to the washroom, and snuck off. Once inside, I stood in front of the mirror. I felt like I was looking at the person I wanted to be, not the person I actually was. I couldn't imagine my folks seeing me in this ridiculous coat. I wondered if I too would change with the gears of time, or if I'd be left behind and forgotten.

When I came back, the house lights flickered twice. "Well, enjoy the main attraction." Gloria winked at Fanny and then smiled at me.

Fanny and I made our way back to our seats for the screening of *9 Lives of a Wet Pussy*. The protagonist, unsatisfied with her love life, sleeps with any man who catches her eye. The first sex scene happens in a gas station bathroom with the man filling up the car opposite her.

In Fanny's first workshop story, a seventeen-year-old hitchhikes from New York City with a briefcase to visit her aunt in Montreal. Up until Plattsburgh, somewhere in between what she already sees as her past life and a fresh start, she's bored by how easy the trip has been. She was yearning for friction, some kind of revelation, some piece of information she hadn't previously accessed. Instead, she makes it to Plattsburg without once taking out her wallet; transport, gas, food, all covered by truckers eager to spend a short while in the company of a young lady.

She decides she wants to spend the night in a hotel with a decent-looking trucker. In the room, lying on the croaking springs of the old motel bed, she doesn't tell him that she's on the pill. He doesn't ask her and fucks her without a condom anyway. When he pulls out, she expects him to finish on her. She closes her eyes, waiting for it to pool in her navel or her suprasternal notch, or spread across her chest. Instead, she opens her eyes after hearing a strained moan, and sees him handing her a mug with an ounce of an opaque milky substance in it. She spends the night on top of the comforter, listening to him snore.

When I questioned some possible plot holes, the other writers looked down at the floor. The instructor's gaze burned a hole in my neck. It was understood that this was fiction, and artifice was key, but all fiction draws from life, and this was a life I knew nothing about. I knew about belt spankings. I knew not to talk about the empty wine bottles in the garage, nor of Mom's stained teeth. I knew what the sound of an opened fridge late at night meant. I knew about sneaking booze into theatres, about letting Mom misspell words during Scrabble. I knew about the other world; the one Fanny hadn't grown up in. We moved on to the next story, but Fanny continued to look at me.

I felt Fanny's hand patting my pocket for the flask again. By the time I remembered that it was still with her, she was unbuckling my belt. I looked over at her face lit up by the light projected on the screen. She was looking at me as she had in that workshop—looking for another story.

Images floated across the screen, and a warm surge rushed my cheeks. I smelled her perfume, or her hand lotion, or her shampoo, or maybe a mix of all three. It smelled like lilac. Fanny leaned in and whispered in my ear, "Couldn't do this in a bar, could we?" She withdrew her hand from my waistband, pulled out a tissue from her purse to clean up, and then handed it to me. I didn't make eye contact when I took it from her. I slid the tissue in my pants, then tossed it on the floor. I wondered if Fanny would like me when she was sober.

We watched the rest of the movie, and I struggled to understand how this theatre still existed in the 21st century. Walking to the theatre before I had met up with Fanny, I had passed a Forever 21, an Urban Outfitters, tattoo parlors, strip clubs, and a Cineplex on the same street. Who pays for porn, and what would the owner do when it closed? We were sitting in a relic—wistful and watching this porno come to an end. I began to miss the place while still sitting in it.

What used to be on this street back when adult theatres were popular? I wondered as we left the theatre and walked along Saint-Laurent Boulevard. We finished the flask and the whole world felt lighter than before. It was snowing—I wrapped my scarf around my neck and watched Fanny veil her silver dress with a beige peacoat. I thought I might have a chance in this life.

"Let's go back to mine," Fanny said. "It's only a ten-minute walk away."

We staggered through the streets and turned off into an alley behind some apartment buildings, arm in arm, steadying ourselves to keep from tipping over. It was nice to have an excuse to be close. She jumped on my back, squeezing her legs around my hips, her arms around my shoulders, and together we passed by a Fisher-Price basketball net.

"*Swish.*" She laughed and then bit my neck. "Put me down. I want to dance."

"What do you want to dance to?"

"Something slow. You choose."

She hopped down, and I pulled my phone out and scrolled through artists. The LED screen lit up my face in the dark, my pupils growing wider in the night. I scrolled onto Leonard Cohen and played "Tonight Will Be Fine." Trees tilted from behind backyard fences, arching over the alley and forming a corridor above the streetlights, and snow seeped through cracks in the sky. The moon hung by a black thread. As we spun around that alley, I pulled her closer and she nestled her head into my collar, breathed into my ear. I imagined the birds from the song perched on the telephone wire.

"Why do you like me?" I asked.

"I'm not convinced I do," she said.

I kept silent. She could tell I was really asking.

"I get something from you."

"So you're using me?"

"What's wrong with that?" she asked. "Relationships are transactional in nature. You use me in your own way. Doesn't mean you don't also like me."

Holding Fanny in my arms, I got to realizing there was so much life I hadn't lived. I looked over her shoulder into the windows of the apartments next to us. In one window, a father was cooking eggs for his two daughters who were both sitting on the counter, legs dangling over the edge. In another room, a lone lady sat on her rocking chair, reading a book by lamplight. A cat brushed up against my leg, and I nearly stepped on it. It hissed and retreated beneath a chain-link fence.

"You remind me of my old life," she said at last.

"Sometimes I feel like I'm from the past," I said.

"Then catch up with the present. And take me on a real date soon."

"What do you think the world will look like when that theatre shuts down?" I asked.

Will be fine, will be fine, will be fine, for a while.

She didn't say anything. We kept dancing and I dipped her, brought her back to me against gravity's will.

"Sadder," she finally said.

"And you think it will shut down?"

"Like a failing organ," she said. "It has to. This relationship will shut down. You will shut down. Ideas shut down. The only thing that keeps going is ideas, and even those get replaced."

After our dance we kept walking and finally got to her apartment. Fanny kept dropping her keys outside the front door and laughing about it. When we did get in, she walked through the corridor in her wet boots, straight to the record player in her living room, and thumbed through her vinyl collection. The snow turned to rain and tapped on the windows. It felt like we had a secret place in the world, like we were locked in our own furtive home. She played *Oscar Peterson For Lovers.* The front door was bolted, and boot prints traced her path from the entrance.

She went to the kitchen and mixed margaritas, while I stood next to the record player in the living room, looking out the window. The warm scratch of vinyl dripped off the walls, and the carpet felt nice beneath my socks. We drank margaritas and listened to the rest of the album from her room. Before the record was over, we were lying on her bed.

We rolled around and she undid my belt buckle. The rain still beat down but on a different window now, and I wondered if our footprints were still in that alley. Her hands kept moving down while I tried to hold her and kiss her neck. I thought of all those old men and what they did for a living. I thought of their bald heads and wondered if my father had ever done anything like that. Fanny's hands were on my skin, but they didn't feel good anymore.

The needle was looping in the final groove, and the theatre was still there after so many years. Snow turned to rain and rain turned to snow. Mothers and fathers cooked dinner for their children. Things stayed the same, but everything changed. You ended up alone reading a book or you died before the ones you loved. Not everybody loved. I held Fanny in my arms, and it really felt like I had something. She took her hand out of my pants.

"You okay?" she asked.

"I'm fine."

She rested her head on my chest. I looked over at the empty glasses.

"I'm sorry. I think I drank too much."

"You're not the first. We can try again in the morning."

We lay on our backs and she lit a cigarette. I cracked the window open and felt the crisp air raise the hairs on my arms. She was still wearing that silver dress.

"I'm going to get naked. You can sleep in my bed if you promise not to take advantage of me while I sleep."

I didn't answer and she slipped her dress off her shoulders and down around her hips. It fell to her ankles. I stayed in my clothes. She passed me the cigarette.

"Goodnight."

She turned off her bedside lamp and got under the covers, and I lay on top of them for a while with my clothes on, finishing the rest of the cigarette. I felt her breathing beside me, heard the rain tapping on the window. I looked up at the ceiling.

The wind blew through the trees outside her window, and a few blocks farther, the theatre lights had already shut off. I thought about all of this, about the woman lying next to me, about what it would be like in the morning. The rain tapped on the window. I lay on top of the sheets. I took off my socks and wondered what the world would look like in another forty years.

The Milk's Gone Sour

I WAS WRITING A PAPER on Virginia Woolf when the telephone rang.

It was an undergraduate English essay on "The Cinema" and I was examining "life as it is when we have no part in it," but really, I hadn't a clue. The TV was playing in the room over, and I could hear it through my bedroom wall. My roommate was watching *The Bugs Bunny Show* on a small television set. I heard the murmur of dialogue playing through the wall, the bottom half of all that was being said.

I reached for the flip phone on my desk but hesitated before picking it up. I couldn't think of anyone I wanted to talk to so decided not to answer. A dog was barking outside. It was winter, and a particularly cold day; I was wearing two sweaters. I looked around my room and closed my laptop, shut the window, cracked my knuckles, and tried to figure out how long I had been at this essay. The television carried through. I thought of a motel room I once stayed in with my younger twin brothers—

everyone around me fast asleep, the sounds of late-night cable porn playing through the walls. Muffled, croaking.

I left my unfinished paper and passed through the living room on my way to the kitchen. My roommate Robbie sat on the couch, eating a bowl of cereal without milk. I stood in the door frame, watching him keeled over laughing with the old wooden floorboards creaking beneath his slippers. The floors dipped toward him. He'd left a depression in the wood through his permanence. My entrance went unnoticed.

I made my way toward the fridge and found that it had been left open. Robbie's eyes were glued to the screen. I heard my phone go off in my room again. It sounded like my alarm clock.

"You going to get that?" he asked through a mouthful of Cheerios.

"You left the fridge open."

I looked at Robbie, who didn't bother answering, then back into the kitchen.

"Why can't you close the fridge," I asked, "or the cupboards or the drawers or anything?"

He cupped the bowl in his palm and spooned the rest of the dry cereal into his mouth. I glanced over at the screen and watched Elmer Fudd aim his rifle at Bugs Bunny and fire off a shot. The rifle exploded in his hands, creating a dark cloud that filled the screen. When the shroud of smoke subsided, his face was covered with a thick layer of soot. A carrot had been lodged in the gun's barrel.

"Didn't use the fridge today," Robbie said. "Must have been you."

I wondered why I had moved in with some guy I didn't know, why I hadn't found a friend who was also moving to Montreal to study. There were so many Robbies in Montreal. At least I had more space than back home, some distance from the twins and Mom.

I let it go and opened the already breached fridge. It emitted warm yellow light onto the black-and-white linoleum floors, sang a faint music, a loud hum. A sour stench spilled from it. I pinched my nose with one hand and rummaged through the shelves with the other, tossing aside the wilting herbs and the package of three-day-old thawed chicken. My hand hovered over the carton of milk. The cow's condescending face looked me in the eyes. *Beware, kid…* it said, laughing. *The milk's gone sour.* I lost my appetite.

The telephone rang, again.

I left the kitchen behind and the milk in the fridge. I got to my room and sat in my chair, listening to Bugs Bunny finish his line before I answered. Two rings after the first. I answered on the fourth. My roommate laughed in the other room when the voice on the phone told me that my sister had killed herself. I think that's what made me most sad. Bugs Bunny was fleeing from Elmer Fudd, my roommate was laughing, the milk was sour, the fridge was humming, and my sister Rose was dead. I hadn't seen her in over a year, and so maybe it was my fault.

Rose and I didn't speak often, though I always thought that this was on account of us saving all our stories for the next time we hung out or had a beer. That image lingered in my head: walking into a tavern, my eyes adjusting from the bright lights outside, focusing on the outline of a body leaning over the bar, an apparition waiting for me on that lonesome stool. I thought the world was cruel for separating us over time. My roommate laughed. He was right.

"Cliff, do you understand what I've just told you?" It was my mom's voice on the other end, but I couldn't hear her very well, so it could have been anyone. Everything sounded muffled, like I was listening to the bottom half of what was being said.

When she told me what my sister had done, I didn't respond. I pictured a flock of seagulls circling a carcass on a beach, a choir of these feathered birds singing. Then, somewhere else, I imagined a newborn baby swaddled in blankets, crying out, adding to that same song, that same Global Atmospheric Circulation. The newborn cried its own chords, its bottom spanked bare as loved ones waited for their turn to hold it in their arms, circled around, releasing their own gasps of admiration, swallowing the songs of birds and newborn life.

Rose never felt too close to any of us, except maybe Viviane. She was always further off, somewhere else. Maybe things might have taken a different course if I had made myself more available. I should have called her more.

Life as it is...

Mom's voice trickled from the receiver as she went on talking. I wanted to hear the television in the next room but what I heard was the dripping voice and the clock ticking next to me. I put the phone down without hanging up. The voice continued buzzing on my desk.

I walked into the living room after hanging up the phone. My roommate was sitting where I last saw him, staring at Elmer Fudd, who was still in pursuit of Bugs Bunny. I sat next to him on the couch and thought it was going to swallow me whole. The walls looked like they had a fresh coat of paint. The TV looked smaller. It was probably time to buy a new couch.

"Who was it?"

"My sister."

"How's she doing?"

"She's alright I guess, just sold one of her paintings."

"Nice, where does she live now?"

"She's living somewhere." I gazed into the shrunken TV screen, sinking further into the couch.

Bugs Bunny tied a stuffed rabbit to the fin of a shark, tricking Fudd into chasing it into the ocean. Fudd hopped into his boat and chased "Bugs Bunny" into the horizon. Shortly into his pursuit, the shark turned and surfaced from below, exposing alabaster arrowhead teeth and a smug grin, swallowing Fudd's boat in a single gulp. Fudd remained suspended in the air. Robbie laughed. Fudd ran to shore for rescue, his legs serving as rotary propellers keeping him above surface, but was kidnapped by pirates along the way. They sailed into a speck on the horizon and Bugs Bunny got away.

It was sad that Bugs Bunny got away. A man with a gun always gets the hare. I wanted the kids to know. I got up to go to the kitchen and opened the cupboard. I found an empty box of cereal. I went to the fridge and picked up the carton of milk to give it a smell. It was pretty bad. I poured myself a glass.

When I was a child, my mother forced me to drink a glass of curdled milk. She thought I was making excuses to avoid drinking it and told me that I wouldn't be excused from the table until I finished it. I drank the first half and became nauseous. When she turned away, Rose took the opportunity to drink the rest. She looked at me and winked, as if to say, *Thanks for the spoiled milk, kid.* She put it back onto the table, chunks of curdled dairy sliding down the sides of the glass. It made sense for me now to do the same.

After I finished my glass, I left the carton on the counter and went back to my room. I sat down where I had taken the call. The phone was where I left it, and I waited.

But it didn't ring. It sat there, as did I, day after day, until somebody called to ask if I had life insurance. It was spring, Robbie had gone back home to Arizona, there was a stack of bowls in the corner of my room. The snow melted to reveal the ground beneath, and somewhere a dead rabbit thawed, its coat of grey fur gone, the carcass slowly disintegrated by the enveloping forest, its bones a championed medallion around Death's collar. And all the while, as life unfolded around me, I remained seated, unsure of what to do with my hands.

I picked up the phone and dialed Rose's number, and I got a strange man's voice on the other end. I told him the story about the sour milk. He stammered, asked who I was and why I was calling him. I told him that my sister Rose and I used to go home after school when we were much younger and sit on the living room floor together to watch Looney Tunes on our box TV. He asked who I was, angrier now, insisting I not prank call this number. I kept recounting similar stories, speaking into the phone long after it had gone quiet.

And How About Them Planes?

It's all very strange when the ones we love are gone. We sit and eat our sandwiches and tell ourselves this isn't happening, not to me. We shower and watch the dirt go down the drain, but the dirt looks different. It's running down someone else's legs. We watch ourselves from above and think, how odd, this can't be happening to me. Not to me.

These thoughts looped around Eleanor Whitehall's head while she looked out at the St. Lawrence River from her Adirondack chair. She took another bite from her tuna sandwich and poured herself a glass of wine. She breathed in through her nose, feeling her belly expand with each inhale as she screwed the cap back onto the bottle.

It was nice to sit and drink, to sit and think. There hadn't been much time for it recently. She felt like she had been awakened from a week-long stupor of reacting, a week of being told what to think and what to do. After this glass of wine, she wouldn't let that happen anymore. She took a sip. The sun was setting as she was waking up. A flock of geese landed, their descending V a reflection on the water that diminished into a slight skip and splash. She was regaining control, and deciding what she would do. She thought about taking another week off from the cheese factory.

There was a bulky telephone on the armrest of her chair. She had brought out the landline—in case of an emergency. As she took off her shoes, it rang.

"Hello?"

"Eleanor?" A man's voice.

"Speaking."

"I was one of Herb's friends." He paused. "We've never met. I wanted to phone and extend my sincerest apologies for your loss. It's been a tough one for me as well, for *all* of us. Herb and I were good friends. I thought it would be nice to talk. For both of us."

She had never heard this man's voice before. She took another sip of wine and thanked him. "How did you know each other?" she asked.

"The aviation club," the man said.

"Right. I'm sorry, what was your name again? My memory's shot."

"That's alright. That's understandable, of course. I'm Robert."

The name didn't sound familiar, but she had never really taken an interest in Herb's aviation club or the model planes he had filed along their shelves and their garage walls. She would drive in after work, park her car, and scan the room from behind the wheel. She'd take a short breath before grabbing her purse and opening the door. She'd dreamed of walls neatly filed with gardening tools, but of course, those renovations had never happened. Instead, Herb had erected displays for his model planes. She would look at them, sitting there on the wall, and then pull her phone out from her purse to see if she had received any messages on the drive home. At their mention now, she heard their plastic engines revving in the stale air.

"Well thank you for calling, Robert. It's nice to speak with someone. I haven't really known what to do with myself recently. I keep telling myself that none of this is real, that I'll wake from this all tomorrow. I have to remind myself that I'm sitting in my house in Bainsville."

"Do you have someone taking care of you?"

"My nephew checks in on me most days, and I still have the sandwiches from the service. They're tuna sandwiches. I've been eating those." She trailed off, wondering if she had said too much, remembering her nephew's face from the funeral. *I'm sorry for your loss, Aunt Eleanor.* She had looked up at him and smiled, with only one corner of her mouth rising. She felt her makeup cracking as it stretched across her skin. *Oh sweetheart, what loss? Is any of this real?* She could still see his contorted face, twisting.

The mosquitoes were getting bad. She considered going in but decided against it; she wanted to be outside, and the mosquitoes wouldn't change that. *Let them bite*, she thought, looking down at her bare feet. They looked like someone else's feet.

"Listen, it's a loss for us all really. It's tough," Robert said. "God permitting, I'd like to take you out for a coffee sometime soon. I'd love to share some stories with you about Herb."

He sounded chipper. She couldn't understand why they hadn't met, but then again, Eleanor had friends that Herb had never met: coworkers from the cheese factory, some friends from bridge. There was even Stanley, the man with a limp whom she met at the community garden a few blocks from their home. She and Stanley got along well; he made her laugh, and he knew about tropical zones and soil acidity. She liked knowing people that Herb didn't personally know. It gave her a slice of her own life, one that wasn't shared.

"You and Herb were good friends, so I don't see why not. He seemed to mean a lot to you."

She was no longer hungry. She tossed her sandwich to the shoreline for the geese to eat. It fell just before the water.

"Thank you, Eleanor. It's a pity we haven't met, though I feel like we have. I've already heard so much about you."

"Will you pick me up? I'm in no condition to drive."

"Well, actually, that's why I'm calling," he admitted.

She sat with a blank expression while her garden lay vacant. There should have been hydrangeas and rose bushes, soil coated in black mulch, taxus hillii yews at the back, fuchsias sloping in the middle for the hummingbirds, fat-faced peonies, Irish moss, geraniums, clovers, and peppery nasturtiums. But they never had room in the garage for the tools.

"Listen," Robert continued, lowering his voice. "I was in the aviation club with Herb, as you know, and he borrowed a few of my model planes as reference for his own similar models. He needed them for a week or two, but the problem is that he passed away before he finished. I know this isn't great timing, but I was hoping to get those back before it's too late. I could stop by and show you which ones."

She took a pause as she blinked. She didn't know much about those planes, but she knew their value. She had watched their joint chequing account take a hit with each new model that arrived at their door in a neatly packaged cardboard box. She felt short of breath.

"I don't know you well, Robert, and I don't know Herb's planes much either, but I knew Herb. He was stubborn as a mule. He wouldn't have borrowed anything from anyone even if it could have helped him."

"I know, I know. I realize this must seem suspicious. I expected this. He told me you didn't know much about his collection, and so I expected some resistance."

His voice cracked on this last word. "Why don't I come by soon and we can go over which models are mine?"

"I don't think you should come."

"Oh, don't take it like *that*, Eleanor. We were friends, good friends." His voice raised an octave higher. "Please, don't make it like this."

Eleanor was becoming more certain that she had never heard of him before. *Robert. What a peculiar name*, she thought. It sounded much too formal, like a man who sat at a desk, not in a cockpit. Now Herb—*that* was a pilot's name. She had never thought about it before, but now she was sure of it. Herb was the name of a man who had his garage lined with shelves of model planes, who studied them and fantasized about them, who relived his days and worked through the polystyrene-plastic-like exposure therapy. A man who didn't only build planes, but who also flew them. Robert was the name of a man who called elderly women for life insurance scams. Who got shat on by geese and called it luck. *Robert*, she thought, *a despicable name*.

As she took the phone with her and walked into the garage, it all felt new. "Now listen," she could hear him backpedalling. "I was in the same squadron as Herb. We were stationed in the 4th Canadian Division Support Base in Petawawa. Would a stranger know that?"

She closed her eyes and pictured Herb sitting on the leather couch in their living room, polishing one of the planes while she washed the dishes. "Now you listen to me, Robert. I know that Herb didn't speak much about his experience in the war, but anyone who spent a few nights with him would know where he was based, *especially* if they were in an aviation club."

She wasn't sure of this but said it anyway. There was a time when everything Herb had told her about his time flying with his dad, or his time in the war, was new and exciting. Once she had heard all the stories several times over, she was happy he had his aviation club so that he could tell them for the first time again. But this was her conversation now and it made her feel closer to Herb. It felt like he was telling her a new story, one he had held onto and surprised her with now. She paced around the garage, excited by the sounds of her own steps echoing off the walls. It no longer mattered that the garden lay bare or the garage full, that her tuna sandwich was souring on the shore. What mattered were the planes around her and the retreating voice in the receiver.

"I can call later then. This probably wasn't the best time. I'll just stop by later to pick up my planes."

"Don't bother."

"I don't understand?" his voice strained.

"Don't. Bother," she repeated, only louder.

"Now listen, I know you're grieving, but this is no way to behave. I know you're sore, but that doesn't change that a man's planes are a man's planes."

She looked around at the models on the wall. His

voice was undulating over the receiver. She read the labels meticulously written under each.

"Of course, Robert. That I can understand. I do apologize. A man's planes *are* a man's planes." She ran her hand through her hair and examined the garage she had driven into twelve thousand times in this life. "Well then, was it the F-14 Tomcat?" she asked.

"Well, no. It wasn't, Eleanor. It wasn't that one."

She took it from the wall and threw it across the room. The impact against the concrete wall was loud enough to be heard over the phone.

"Was it the Thunderbolt II?"

"Uhh, no, Eleanor," he stammered. "That one isn't mine."

She hurled it on the floor. A piece of shrapnel shot up and grazed her cheek. *This is war*, she thought, *and pilots get hurt.*

"Well, Robert, I'm having quite the difficult time finding your model planes then."

He was breathing heavy. She heard it.

"Eleanor," he projected, "this is no way to act toward your husband's *friend.* I simply want my models back and you are acting… *ecstatic.*"

She stood in the garage and started laughing.

"*Please…*" he said.

She laughed louder. She moved the receiver away from her ear and her hands began to shake. The surrounding planes made her think of propellers splitting the air, of the dust kicked up from the ground. She saw herself from above. She was a pilot. No, she was a lady laughing in her garage. She was both.

"Now listen," he said.

Her voice grew louder, and she hurled vicious remarks at him as she left the garage and paced through her living room. She passed framed pictures of Herb and herself, of Herb and members of the aviation club. None of them looked like Roberts. She was landing, descending back into herself. Robert trailed on and she hung up the phone.

She calmly walked upstairs and landed on the plush pillow, onto the soft comforter of her bed, and finally lay still. She could hear her heart beating. She could hear her pulse too. She began to slow her breath, listening for the sounds of geese in her backyard. Images from the funeral earlier that day ran through her head. Only the aviation club and a few family members had shown up for Herb. There wasn't a Robert there.

A Sensitive Man Drinks Yellow Flowers

A PLANK OF WOOD props open the kitchen window in my apartment, where the rush-hour traffic echoes off the shelves and an exposed lightbulb covers my father in warm light, even though he looks so cold. I haven't seen him in over ten years and now we are drinking bottles of yellow beer in my kitchen.

"Would you shut that thing, Seymour?" A cloud forms on his breath and he points at the window.

"Can I see it?"

"Once you shut it. Please."

Sitting at my kitchen table, he draws his coat to cover his chest. His face is like the wilted end of a dying cigarette. I wait a while longer, and watch him shiver. I am straddling the window ledge, smoking a cigarette, my left leg dangling down from the third floor of my apartment building. The alley below is coated in a fresh layer of snow. In the neighbouring building a father disappears from one window and reappears in the next, leaving a trail of darkness behind him. In the next room his family sits together in TV light.

"Alright," I say, standing up and closing the window behind me. "Show me."

My father stands up and pulls his tuque over his ears, then removes his winter coat and drapes it over the back of his chair. Next, one by one, the buttons of his shirt. A button pops off and rolls across the floor like a marble. He stands in front of me with his shirt pulled apart, exposing his bare chest. The hair has begun to grow back since the quadruple bypass surgery, but the white cotton of his dress shirt is similar to his skin tone. Along the middle of his chest, a raised pink scar runs lengthwise. He looks like he's been welded shut. I want to reach out and run my finger along it.

"Does it hurt?"

"Not so much anymore." He buttons up his shirt, skipping the missing button. "I'm supposed to take it easy for a while longer. It's only been four weeks, recovery is usually six to twelve."

After redressing, he sits back in his chair and tells me the story he has come here to tell me: the minor chest pains, the routine checkup, the doctors' sudden and severe attention, their springing into stoic action after discovering the blocked arteries, his being rushed into ICU, the open-heart surgery, the days spent on a gurney, the overemphasis at his luck for having caught it when they did.

He picks up his beer and puts it back down without drinking from it. Though he's hardly taken a sip, I walk over to the fridge and pop open a second bottle of Molson Export for myself. Brown bottles, yellow beer. *Half fart, half horse piss, all wonderful yellow flowers,* I titter.

The man sitting in front of me in this half-light is not my real father. Not really. This man is much softer. I wonder if I could come to know him, if we might learn another way of communicating. My real father once stalked and hunted me down our street. He sat me down on our front porch after Thanksgiving dinner to lecture me about table manners. When I told him I understood and that he was repeating himself, when I got up to walk away, he yanked my arm so hard I fell to the ground. I got up off the floor and I ran away, and he chased me. He drove his shoulder into my back and my vision went black, my body pressed between his body and the pavement. I heard my mother screaming from the porch. He picked me up by the belt of my pants—my chafed cheek bleeding from sliding across the pavement and my eye already swelling—and dragged me home like an overstuffed suitcase. He tossed me on the vestibule floor, slammed the door, and I waited on the cold tiles before getting up, making sure he wouldn't come back, listening to him and my mom shouting at each other.

If that man and the man in front me are the same, then there are ways in which they are different. This man isn't clean-shaven for one. His face has sprouted grey stubble. For the first time, I weigh more than him. He's still broad shouldered and over six foot, but he's lost maybe thirty pounds. I wonder if I could take him in a fight now, if I could outrun him, if I could tackle him to the ground. It could still go either way. He's fifty-five, but I estimate that in another ten years I'll cross over into a new stage in life, a period where for the rest of his life I'll be able to beat him. The simple arithmetic of violence. It's difficult to reconcile the man I knew growing up with the man sitting across the table from me.

Upstairs, someone stomps across the floor. It must be Artie, my upstairs neighbour, who I haven't seen in a few days. "Noisy neighbours," he says, looking up at the cracked paint on the ceiling and wincing at noticing it.

"I don't mind. It's nice to hear the human sounds of people living around you. Plus I have to like it. I can't afford to rent one of those new-build condos in Griffintown or Little Burgundy."

"Right, well if you ever need any help—"

I cut him off. "I've got it covered, thanks. I like this neighbourhood anyway. It's a significant neighbourhood. Do you know *why* this neighbourhood is significant?" He shakes his head, though I already know the answer to my question. "Because St. Henri is where your grandfather, *my* great-grandfather, Liam Murphy, first lived when *his* father, Connor Murphy, decided to move here from Ireland in 1901. They lived a few streets over from here, on de Courcelle Street. Your great-grandfather was a yardmaster for CN Rail. Did you know any of that?"

The same shake of the head, but I knew that too. I'm pushing him, taking on the tone I use when lecturing to my students, seeing if he'll bite and if that temper will boil up again. My father never told me anything about his family growing up. I always felt like I was born from a void. He made a point of not bringing it up, and whenever I asked him about it, he would deflect or claim ignorance.

But nothing. No sharp edges, no irritation, no cutting tone, and certainly no interest. "I didn't know my father too well." He shifts in his chair, looking more uncomfortable than irritated. "So I don't know much about all of that. Was never interested in that stuff."

"Well I was always interested in it," I say.

I don't know what my grandfather looks like; I've never seen a picture of him, not even in my genealogical research. Either there were no pictures of him or they've been discarded and destroyed. The story I've stitched together over my life, the piecemeal account is that my grandfather left my grandmother and their six kids when my father was ten. My grandmother worked as a nurse and raised my father and his five siblings by herself. Before my grandfather left them, he worked as a professor of history at several Montreal CEGEPs—a complete coincidence I only learned of after becoming one myself. He also sold weed out of their garage, which mellowed his temper, but he drank a lot too, which brought it back up. This narrative was largely gathered from my aunts and uncles. My father and I had never really found a way to connect or talk about these things, or much else.

I don't know if my grandfather's alive or not. I've never spoken with him. When I moved out at eighteen, my aunt told me that I looked like my grandfather, that I reminded her of him, that I had his red hair and his independence, which is when I realized that I must remind my father of him too. I was never like my father, though I had to come from somewhere. But that was ten years ago now.

"So, you were dead?" I stand back up and light another cigarette.

"They have a machine pumping oxygen into your blood so the heart remains still." The room feels stale with no machine pumping oxygen into it. I open the window again, sit on the ledge.

"So, you were dead."

"Depends on how you look at it." He shifts in his seat. "Assisted living is more accurate. But I could have been, which is why I wanted to see you." He pauses. "Do you mind if I use your washroom?"

"It's down the hall."

He pushes his chair from the table and gets up to leave. As he's getting up, I want to stop him from leaving, to reach across the room and tug on his sleeve like the string of a kite. I want to forgive him, but that's not quite right. I want to know why I want to forgive him, why I agreed to see him, and I feel like I can only answer that question while looking at him. His presence is the necessary precondition. This feeling leaves just as soon as it arrives. He tells me he'll be quick, and I sit in the kitchen, listening to the world beat through the open window.

Before I get up from my chair to crack a third bottle of yellow beer, I hear Fanny's key in the back door. The door swings open into the kitchen and our cat Tabitha comes running in from the fire escape between Fanny's legs, patrolling the apartment before making her way to her bowl of water. Fanny carries two brown paper bags of groceries, stalks of celery towering out from the top of one. She kicks the door shut behind her.

"*I'm sorry*," she whispers and kisses me. "Is he still here?"

"Just in the washroom. Don't apologize. It's your apartment too." I get up to help her with the groceries.

"I'll leave as soon as I drop these off. I thought I would be out for longer, but it's so cold out there I couldn't wait."

"I'm glad you're here."

I met Fanny in a creative writing workshop in university. I never intended to pursue writing, but I always thought she would. In some ways she did—she loved language, she employed it better than anyone I knew, she understood its roots, where it came from, but she decided other people's words were of greater value, so she became a freelance translator, mostly translating

French books into English, while occasionally taking corporate contracts.

When my father returns, he looks surprised to see Fanny. My mom told me she had mentioned Fanny over a phone call with him so he was aware of her existence, but I don't think he was expecting to see her for the same reasons I hadn't intended on introducing them. I don't want to let him into my life beyond my kitchen.

"Mr. Murphy, it's nice to meet you." Fanny wipes her hands off and shakes his. "I'm Fanny."

"Yes, I've heard of you. Great to meet you, Fanny!" My father is suddenly upbeat, full of charm. "Please, call me Henry." He is smiling his thin-lipped smile.

"I won't be staying. I don't want to interrupt your time together. Can I make you a pot of tea before I go?"

"*Yes,* please!" My father jumps at the offer as if he'd been deprived. "Decaf, if you don't mind."

Fanny fills the stovetop kettle in the sink, and as my father lowers himself into his seat she turns over her shoulder with an apologetic look. I smile at her. She is too kind not to offer. Asking her not to be would be asking her not to be herself, and I won't let anyone do that.

"Is chamomile alright?" she asks.

"My favourite." He smiles.

Fanny pulls up a chair and sits with us at the table. Before the kettle boils, my father asks her more questions about herself than he's asked me in my entire life. I get up to ration two teaspoons of dried flowers into a strainer, fetch a tea cup and saucer from our display shelf, and try not to feel disappointed or jealous. The water is bubbling, and within a few minutes the boiling kettle whistles into the room.

"Well, I'll go seek refuge upstairs at Artie's for a bit," Fanny says, getting up to take the kettle off the burner. "Do you know if he's home, Seymour?"

"If he lives upstairs," my dad interrupts, "then I can assure you he is."

We all three laugh, and for a moment I feel like I am watching this scene play out from outside, looking in through the window from the building across the alleyway: the three of us huddled around a steaming cup of yellow tea, the steam rising up in a cone of light, all of us in our winter coats. I feel the tingling warmth of alcohol across my chest, and for a moment I want to forgive him before he's asked.

"Thank you for the tea, Fanny. I hope to see you again." He gets up and shakes her hand again. Fanny comes over and hugs me from behind, then leaves from the same door she came in, a cold draft replacing her. The remnants of Fanny's presence linger in the room: steam rising out from the neck of the kettle, an emptied bowl on the counter now filled with bananas, the loneliness and stillness of an empty room that was just full.

"You know," my father says, looking at me, still bathed in all that warm yellow light. "I'm glad you agreed to see me. Your mother's told me you're doing very well. She says you're very young to already be a professor."

I nod, finish my beer and fetch myself a fourth. "Do you and Mom speak often?" They got a divorce after I left home, a whole world undone that I wasn't around to witness.

"I call to ask about you. Not too much else to say." If the father I grew up with said this, I wouldn't have believed him. But this man is not my father, not exactly. "You know, when I was lying in the gurney before my surgery, I kept thinking of my favourite memory of us. I don't think I've ever told you about it." He looks at me as if to confirm, or to wait for me to ask.

"Which one?"

"Do you remember when we used to go to Centennial Park in the winter to go tobogganing?"

"Yeah, we had that sled with the steering wheel and the yellow metal frame."

"That's the one… Well, for a couple of years you were terrified—you would brake all the way down the hill, and I had to push you down, for you to do it. I remember thinking, *Wow, my son's a pansy.* You know? Like, how's he going to get through life? You were always quiet and reading, a real shy type, always looking at your shoes, couldn't look people in the eye. But then one year, you must have been eight or nine, we hiked up the hill for the first time that winter. I thought I'd have to push you down, but once we got to the top of the hill, you jumped on the toboggan and shot off and steered toward the line of people hiking up the hill! You were like a bowling ball. They all dove out of the way!"

He interrupts his own story with a fit of coughing, then begins laughing.

"I couldn't believe what I was watching. I had to apologize to everyone as they came up, and the whole time while I'm waiting for you to walk back up with the sled, I'm trying to understand what happened. It was like I had a new son all of a sudden. When you finally got to the top of the hill, I asked you why you did that, and you said, and I'm quoting here, *I'm crazy, Dad, I'm crazy!* I had been embarrassed before, but right then I had never been so proud. You were fearless."

He's looking at me and nodding. I wait for something more but realize that this is the story. I am trying to translate what he means, why this is his favourite memory. *You have to be fearless to get by in this life, son,* or, *You have to be tough to be someone. You have to knock other people down to get up.* I'm disappointed that this is his favourite memory of us, that up until that point he had been disappointed in me and thought that I wasn't tough enough to get by. I'm angry that he was applying that logic to me as an eight-year-old, but it aligns with everything else about the way he was. I'm even more disappointed that this is *still* his favourite memory. I don't think in those terms—but I know he does, and I can't help but want to live up to them without believing in them. I feel myself compromising to meet him where he is, to adjust. But also, I would be lying if the story didn't make me a little proud. I want to be fearless.

He pulls his tuque over his forehead and bunches up the lapels on his jacket. Here is my father, appearing out of the marsh of ten lost years, trying to teach me another lesson. I wonder what would happen if I got up to leave, if he might grab my wrist and yank me down, what I would do to him if he did.

"Well, I've taken up enough of your time. I should be heading out," he says. "Could I use the washroom again?"

"You know where to find it." As he gets up, I hear Fanny and Artie laughing upstairs. He leaves the room. Despite all the changes that unfold, there are always constants. A lonely kitchen table. I will always have a lonely kitchen table.

"I'll never read a book in translation." Artie exhales and passes the joint to Fanny. "It's like watching a movie with subtitles, or watching a man undress through an eye mask."

Fanny takes it from his fingers. "You're a pervert *and* a moron. That doesn't even make sense," she says.

I am sitting silently on a bean bag, already too high, watching the two of them converse. Every Wednesday we take turns hosting a dinner, and Artie's apartment is filled with items he's stolen from movie sets that he's worked on over the years. My eyes can't land on anything for too long. A large glass terrarium filled with a baseball glove, a bong, and a porcelain statue of the Buddha. A Moroccan rug. A storefront mannequin in a sequin dress. A lamp with a beige lampshade, scenes from a group orgy sketched on each panel in black sharpie, *Libertine Lampshade* written across the top, the lightbulb beneath painted red.

"Despite being dismissive of my work, which I can live with, you're missing out on so many lives, which I can't live with." Fanny takes another hit and offers it to me, but I shake my head.

"What about you, Silent Seymour? What do you think?" Artie springs up from the sofa and walks into the adjoining kitchen as he asks me. In his slenderness, he navigates rooms fluidly, grabbing glasses off of shelves that seem to be out of reach—a fluidity acquired through bartending—then slides back in his languid chair, scrawny legs splayed and one foot propped up on the coffee table. It's how he got the moniker "Arachnid Artie"—all limbs. He pours three whiskeys while staring at me, his Adderall-focused eyes bulging. His wiry hair suggests a man who seldom sleeps. His sleeves and corduroy pants are rolled up to reveal bright yellow socks, and a pack of smokes are tucked into his left sleeve.

"Everything is a translation. Language is a translation of the material into immaterial symbols, expression the translation of thought into sound, so if you're not going to read translations, then why stop at books? You might as well practice your vow of silence and stop thinking, too."

"Listen to the Professor over here." Artie slaps his knee. "Class is in session, Fanny. Did you tell him that?"

"I might have influenced his mode of thinking," she says.

"Besides," I carry on, "surely you've acted in a translated play? Weren't you in *Uncle Vanya*?"

"What I do in my personal life is separate from my professional life." Artie takes a hit and I accept it when he passes it to me. "Everyone has to be a whore occasionally, unless you want to live like Diogenes. Speaking of cleared minds, what's on yours? You're distracted."

"His mom asked him if he'd see his father," Fanny answers as she gets up to sit on the bean bag beside me. "They were just downstairs earlier."

"And?" He sips his whiskey.

"I agreed only because he'd had a medical scare, came close to dying."

"Well you're a better man than I. I'm not sure I'd do the same after everything you've told me. Reminds me a bit of my father."

"I just don't know what I have to say after all this time, what *he* has to say... I haven't seen him in ten years. After an hour in the kitchen, I don't know that we need to reconnect. He's not exactly the conversational type."

"Men of that age usually aren't," Artie says and crosses his leg, his pants hiking up as he does. "What happened?"

"Nothing happened. It's like he was cut off from himself, couldn't actually tell me what he felt." I point at Artie's socks. "Growing up..." I change the subject. "One of his favourite anecdotes was about yellow socks. It was supposed to be a lesson of sorts. When his business started doing well, one of his partners started buying these flashy suits and yellow socks, and whenever he wore them my father would come home and sit me down and tell me that if I ever became successful, that I should never wear yellow socks."

"Ha!" Artie draws a pen and a notepad from his back pocket. "I hope you don't mind. I need to write that down." He is jotting it down before I have time to respond. "It reminds me of that poem you sent me last week, the Al Purdy poem, 'At The Quinte Hotel.' It's got those lines, "*you can see that I am a sensitive man, and I notice the bartender is a sensitive man too, so I tell him about his beer, tell him the beer he draws is half fart and half horse piss, and all wonderful yellow flowers.* Maybe your father was more of a sensitive man than you thought."

Fanny runs her hand through my hair and glances at me. Artie is still writing after a minute, and doesn't once look up at us. In addition to acting, Artie is trying his hand at playwriting, and has the tendency to stop whatever he's doing to write whenever inspiration strikes. It could be during a lunch, in the middle of the street, or the middle of a conversation. In some ways I admire it, but I'm a little pissed off now at being the subject. It's sensitive material, and he is being a little insensitive. There are times where Artie is sheer entertainment, and others where he is caught in his own world, but Fanny and I agreed to be neighbourly, to actually know our neighbours. Neither of us grew up knowing our neighbours; our parents never spoke with them. We wanted to change that.

"We're going to let ourselves out, Artie," Fanny says.

"*Mmmmhmmm*, thanks for the night." He doesn't look up, continues scribbling.

Fanny and I get up from the bean bag and quietly let ourselves out his back door, heading down the fire escape back to ours.

But something did happen before I went upstairs to join Artie and Fanny. I was sitting on the bed, waiting for my father to finish up in the washroom and say goodbye. I'd had a few drinks, and I was drunk on all those warm yellow flowers. In a rare moment of sentimentality, my cat Tabitha pressed up against my shin, looking for attention and affection, and when I didn't pet her, she went looking for it elsewhere, brushing up against the bookshelf. Love pervades all moments if one's eyes are open; or perhaps it's convenience, and Tabitha had an itch.

My father stood in the doorway, the shallow dark hallway behind him. He lingered, standing in between the two rooms. "Can I sit?"

I gestured toward the empty spot on the bed. He sat down beside me, leaving a gap between us. His lapels were drawn together, the button on his coat still fastened, the fabric pulling tight across his chest.

"There's no excuse, I know..." he said, his voice splitting the awkward silence open. He tried to finish his sentence, but instead he bowed his head and held it in his hands.

I wanted to reach across the distance and unbutton his coat for him, relieve all that tension across his chest, for in that moment, I believed it was making him cry.

"There are good reasons but no good excuses, Seymour." Between his tears, he was finally telling me what he had wanted to tell me. Yellow flowers are yellow flowers, and beer is simply beer. "I want you to know I feel regret for how I was. I didn't have a father, and I was trying to figure it out. I was angry at so much."

"It's okay, Dad."

"Your mother is the best, Seymour. You should only love out of love, not out of fear or obligation. Sometimes we need to be selfish, take care of ourselves."

"It's okay, Dad. It's okay."

"You get to a point in your life, Seymour, where you ask yourself, what do I need to do to finally be happy?"

I hope he finds out, the sad slouching man on my bed, a man I do not pity. I hope that he finds the answers to his questions. I wanted to tell him that I love him, that I do not hate him, that I understand. But I couldn't get myself to say the words.

This man sitting beside me from now on is not my father. He is much softer. I wonder if I could come to know this man. I want to hate him, and I want to understand him, too. I want to reach across the room and pull back his coat, unsew the stitches, dig my fingers into the pink ridge of scar tissue, and see what finally comes out.

Raising James Dean

When I was thirteen, I raised James Dean from the dead.

On school nights, when my parents fell asleep, I'd slip out of my cotton sheets, kneel on the carpet, and pray to the wood-framed poster of *Rebel Without a Cause* hanging on my wall. I'd close my eyes and dream of James Dean animated digit by twitching digit, stretching back to sudden life in his red Harrington jacket, slicking back his brown hair, and winking as he stepped out from inside the frame.

The poster was a birthday gift from my older brother Corey. He loved James Dean, and I think he bought it for himself as much as he did for me. I was thirteen and didn't know what I liked yet. Corey had convictions. He seemed so sure of everything and surer still that everyone else should like what he liked. I idolized him. Sometimes I prayed to James, and other times I closed my eyes and pictured Corey on the poster.

He gifted it to me in August of 1999, and that September he moved out of our suburban home in the West Island to study literature at McGill downtown. The poster was a stand-in for what he had taught me, he said, a marker of my first year as a teen. He was my older brother, and I think he assumed responsibility for introducing me to things. That summer we sat on our brown leather couch in the living room several evenings a week, and while I watched *Rebel Without a Cause* on our box TV set, he watched me, pausing the film and rewinding important scenes if I wasn't paying attention. James Dean would stand back up in reverse, let go of his hair, and then resume at a regular pace.

After the movie, no matter how many times we had watched it, he asked me what it was about. I had learned to recite the response. It was about making your own way in life, not conforming to societal pressures, but it was also about a new form of masculinity. I'd parrot the words he used, and even when I answered correctly, he still repeated for emphasis. The movie was meant to break the mould, a man could express himself without following his father's path. He could make his own way in life.

Corey left at the end of the summer, his Hyundai packed with a coat rack sticking out of the back window, and a mattress tied down to the roof rack. He told me to be good, that he'd call every week and that I could take the 470 bus to visit him in the city whenever I wanted. He patted me on the shoulder. I stood on the front steps as his car pulled out of the driveway and disappeared past the corner of our street. I was on my own now. Everything would be up to me.

That was when I decided to raise James Dean from the dead.

The only person I could share all of this with was Catherine. She was my assigned locker neighbour and by no coincidence my only friend at school. As those crucial first weeks passed, we watched groups of friends form and divide into cliques. We didn't manage to successfully break into any. We formed our own twosome and claimed the end of a long table in the corner of the cafeteria. I told her about Corey and about praying to the poster.

"You should wait for a full moon," she said, sitting across from me, biting into her crustless cucumber sandwich. "That's when these paranormal things happen."

I played it cool and nodded, as if that were a perfectly normal conclusion that I might have come to on my own.

"There's one next week."

On the following Monday, I asked my parents for ten dollars for the fall Terry Fox school fundraiser. I hid the bill in my shoe and played hooky the next day. I took a bus to the Salvation Army, where I browsed the aisles and slipped past an elderly woman plugging in all the fans to see if they worked. I bought a red leather jacket for $7.50 and tipped two dollars to Goodwill, for luck. I picked up a couple of red wax candles with the extra fifty cents. I wore the jacket on the way home, pretending to be a young JD.

When I got home, I folded the jacket and hid it with the candles in the hamper in my closet, slipped back into my pyjamas, and when I heard the garage door opening a few hours later, I did push ups until I was feverish and flush with sweat so Mom would think I was sick. It took twenty-five push-ups. I thought James Dean would be proud. I winked at the poster.

Thursday evening, the night of the full moon, I placed the candles on the dresser, the armoire, and the floor, lit them with a match, cracked the window open, got on my knees at the altar of the poster, and just loud enough so he could hear—but quiet enough so as not to wake my parents—uttered the only mantra I could think of: "*You're tearing me apaaaaaaaaart.*"

I did this thirteen, fourteen, fifteen times; I was flush with sweat and fell into a trance. I must have uttered it another fifty times. When I finally opened my eyes, the only thing in the room that had changed was that the candles had burned halfway through their wicks. James Dean was still laminated ink on a sheet of paper. Disappointed, I folded the jacket and put it back in the hamper with the still-warm candles. My cat pushed open my bedroom door to watch the rushed mayhem of my shamed clean-up. I fell asleep alone, James Dean on the wall.

I woke up at 5:30, an hour earlier than my alarm. Some-thing was rustling. I tried to locate the sound within the room. When I pulled open the closet doors, a baby with the head of James Dean was lightly stirring in the hamper, nestled in the jacket.

Instinctively, I picked him up. He was heavy, not a newborn. Maybe a year old. He was strong, too, able to hold his own head up. His eyes shot open, and I worried he would wake up and cry, so I wrapped him back up in the jacket and placed him back in the hamper. The room was still lit by the full moon. Unsure of what to do, I crept into the kitchen and stole the bag of milk from the fridge. I poured some into my old sippy cup that my mom had kept in the basement, and brought it back to my room and was able to get JD to drink some. As long as he slept through the morning, there was no risk of him crying while my parents were getting ready for work. I was still "sick" so I could stay home and invite Catherine over after school. She had better sensibilities about what to do in situations like these, and I trusted her judgment more than my own. It was a Friday, so we could hatch a plan for the weekend.

I remember Catherine's reaction from that Friday afternoon perfectly. I've remembered it ever since. She stood in front of the hamper, wearing her sleeveless vest and stockings, her glasses removed and sitting atop her hair. She looked at me, then the toddler who seemed to have aged a year overnight, then back to me.

"Noah…"

She picked up James Dean and held him at arm's length, inspecting him. His face was unmistakably the actor's, but he didn't seem to know this yet. He looked to be about two now, going on three.

"I can't even get myself to care about *how*," she said, "because we need to figure out *what now*. You can't raise a toddler by yourself. You've just brought a life into this world, Noah. You need to tell someone."

"Not yet." I grabbed her shoulders and led her to my bed, then sat next to her. "We can raise him for now, like parents. He'll need that." James planted his feet on her lap and was standing with her help. He played with strands of her hair.

I had developed a bit of a crush on Catherine. I wasn't planning on telling her because I didn't want to risk ruining our friendship if she didn't feel the same way, and though it was never my intention to coerce her into raising a child together, I secretly took pleasure in imagining it. What would it be like to wake up next to her, to see her in her nightwear, to shower together, to watch her undress? I pushed those thoughts away. Maybe raising James Dean would take us beyond friendship, make us a couple. I knew she wouldn't abandon me on this.

"Okay," she relented, having already done the calculations in her head. "Until we figure out what to do, we'll keep this a secret. But we're going to have to tell someone eventually."

"Sure, yes, of course." I wasn't even thinking about the future. I was raising a child with Catherine, and when he was grown, I'd have a new friend. I could learn from James like I had from Corey, and Corey might even come back more often when he found out about James Dean. I was thrilled and would have danced around the room if it was only me and JD. "Besides, he's growing up fast. I think he ages like a year every day."

"He does seem to be a couple years old," she agreed. "But I'm serious, Noah. We need a plan."

I assured her that my parents thought I had the flu, and I could take another sick week, so we'd have the weekend, next week, and then the following weekend. She could come by after school to check in. By the end of that time, he'd probably be our age if he kept growing at the same rate, and then it would be easier to deal with him. We put JD back in the closet hamper and went to stock up on supplies. We filled our backpacks at the Loblaws down my street. He already had quite a few teeth, which he flashed with his charming smile, so we got some soft fruit and vegetables, granola bars, a rotisserie chicken we'd cut up, and cartons of milk.

We unloaded the provisions into the fridge and went back upstairs. James was peaceful, one of those kids who seems happy to be by themselves. Thankfully, he wasn't much of a crier. Catherine picked him up once more. She rocked him, looking at his face, letting herself grin. "I do get it, though." She kissed him on the forehead. "Why he was such a heartthrob."

JD giggled and said, "Cat-rin."

"His first word!" She laughed and hugged him. I watched them embrace, and it made me feel warm inside. We were a happy family.

"You promise you'll find a way to get help?" she asked, bouncing our young JD up and down on her knee.

"I promise. He can stay in our shed for now. I'll get supplies from the attic, stuff my mom stored from when we were kids. A playpen for the day, so he can't get away, toys, a crib. My parents never go in the shed. I'll tell my brother soon and he'll be able to help."

"You're sure about the shed? Okay, I'll come back early next week." Catherine placed JD between us on the bed and took my hand, then didn't seem to know why she had. She pulled it away and said goodbye. We passed through the house and I watched from the front door as she walked down my driveway, looking back at me to wave, then turned onto the street and disappeared beyond our cedars. What we had was perfect. I knew it would be that much better if we had two.

If I could raise James Dean from the dead, well, I might as well bring someone else back. The next evening, after my parents and James were asleep, I hoisted myself out of my dormer window, shimmied along the window ledge in my pyjama pants, scaled the ridged A-frame onto the roof, then sat cross-legged under the practically full moon of a suburban Saturday night. I closed my eyes and thought of Allen Ginsberg.

Corey had called the house last week. I waited patiently as my mom took her turn on the phone, then my dad, then finally me. I could tell he was excited about university. He asked me how high school was, but after I replied that I was "good," he began ranting about the freedom of university, how no one hovers over you, and how he was learning so much in his literature courses. He began crowing about the "uninhibited genius of Ginsberg." He read a poem to me over the phone where Allen Ginsberg conjures an aisle-browsing Walt Whitman thumbing soft fruits in a grocery store. After the call he said he'd probably be back in a few weeks to visit. I heard a girl's voice in the background and asked who it was, but he quickly said he had to go and said goodbye.

I shut my eyes, balled my hands into fists, and pictured Allen Ginsberg eating a banana in our kitchen. When I opened my eyes, the stars were still blinking at me, and nothing seemed to have changed. I peeked down in the backyard, where the shed remained undisturbed, and where JD slept in his crib. I climbed back down into my bedroom and went back to bed, where I had a dream that our cat was licking my face. I woke up to a full-grown Allen Ginsberg sitting at my bedside, lapping at my cheek. I wasn't startled. Somewhere inside, I always knew if I did it once, I could do it twice. The licking, however, I hadn't anticipated.

"Hey, young Jimbo." His large pupils, so close to mine, were lit by the moon's spotlight, which powered through my bedroom window where undecided curtains billowed in and out of the room. His breath was hot. I held mine. "I was in some deep, long sleep or psychedelic trance, Jimbo. I don't know which one, but there I was sitting in a circle with Kerouac singing the Hare Krishna for some years and then God was there, but no one was surprised, and then God started singing the Hare Krishna, and we were all surprised. I woke up here, or sobered up, and saw that you seemed to be in some horrible nightmarish state, all sweaty and muttering, and so I decided to wake you and clean all that sweat off your face."

I told him to hush, then opened my bedroom door as quietly as I could. Wishing I'd done more research into who Ginsberg actually was, I told Allen to follow me out into the hallway toward the backdoor. We crept along the corridors, old wooden floorboards creaking beneath our feet. On the way out, I stopped off in the kitchen to pick up some bananas and a carton of milk. We tip-toed like shadows across the backyard to the shed, and inside I introduced Allen to JD.

"Say, *look at that!* Did some poor dame shag James Dean?"

"I need you to listen."

Allen was now sitting on a workbench, bouncing JD on his knee. He seemed nonplussed by his own sudden re-entrance into the world. I'm not sure he was convinced he ever left. I explained that they would have to lay low for a while, that I would bring them food and drinks every day until I figured things out. Allen wasn't willing to comply until I promised him some weed, pornographic magazines, and an iPod and headphones. I told him I could get those things in a day or so, once I'd spoken to Corey.

I had tried to tell Corey about JD during our phone call last week, but he was so excited about university that he hardly stopped talking. My parents had been standing near the landline and might have heard, or at least asked what was going on if they heard me whispering. Now, with a full-grown Ginsberg in the picture, I had no choice. Part of me wanted to prove to Corey and Catherine that I could handle it on my own.

I bid Allen and JD goodnight and crossed the lawn like the headlights of a passing car, then slunk back into bed. Now that I had accepted I would have to tell Corey, I got excited about the prospect of it. He'd be thrilled that I had done this for him, that I brought them back for him. Maybe we could all move into his apartment together. I drifted off to sleep, imagining the four of us drinking beer at night, going to bed whenever we wanted.

"You did *what*? With *who?!*"

I explained everything to Catherine on the sidewalk.

She had strips of sunscreen under her eyes. It was now Tuesday, and JD looked to be about six years old. Allen Ginsberg was still the same age. They were waiting for us in the shed.

"You said I should get help. I couldn't tell anyone yet, not even Corey. This was the only solution I could think of."

A few cars drove past my house. School was over for the day, but it was still before 5 p.m. Even during working hours, I was paranoid one of my parents might drive by and see me standing outside when I was supposed to be sick in bed.

"Noah, I don't believe you. Why couldn't you tell Corey? You've just brought a *second* life into this world." She was massaging her temples. The stress made her look older and more beautiful.

I imagined a future with her, both of us at our kitchen table, labouring over our taxes. I'd get up and stand behind her chair to massage her neck, then make us a cup of tea.

"That's only amplified the problem. And why *him*?! Don't you know about his reputation? I mean James Dean I guess I can understand, but I can't believe you'd revive someone so… *problematic*."

I had heard that word before and I still wasn't entirely sure what it meant. I knew it meant that the person had done something wrong, and that because of that wrong thing, you were not meant to like them anymore. Corey had a friend named Frenchie—or maybe that was just his nickname—who eventually stopped coming over. Supposedly whenever Frenchie and Corey went out to the bar he'd immediately go up to every girl in the bar and ask them one after the other if they wanted to go home with him. After they all said no, he'd drink a beer and do it again. After a few beers, he'd do it all over and pinch their arms if they said no. When I asked why Frenchie didn't come over anymore, Corey told me he was problematic.

"What do you mean?!" I said.

"I heard he took advantage of his power to influence underage boys into…well, *stuff*."

"How do you know any of that? How do you even know who he is?" I couldn't believe it. She was wrong. I would have heard about it; my brother would have told me.

"You have one older brother, Noah. I have *three* older sisters and two older brothers. Think about that."

"Just come with me, Catherine. You need to meet him."

I took her hand and she relented, allowing me to pull her along the side of the house past the spigot, the coiled, shrinkable garden hose, and into the backyard. I opened the door to the shed.

James Dean was sitting upright on the workbench with his legs dangling off the edge and playing with a hammer. Catherine rushed over to him and threw the hammer on the floor. Allen Ginsberg was sleeping in the wheelbarrow, with a pair of sunglasses on. He must have felt the fresh breeze come in with us, or heard the clanging of the hammer. He woke up and took his glasses off to survey the room, and when he noticed our presence, his eyes shot open, and he stood up.

"Pardon my manners," he said, standing stiff with his arms at his sides. "I didn't know we were expecting a guest. I didn't know we were *allowed* guests." He bowed, took Catherine's hand, kissed it, and introduced himself as if he weren't Allen Ginsberg. She didn't bother pretending to be honoured or starstuck. She looked horrified by the scene we had walked in on, and she couldn't mask her disgust.

"We're not allowed guests," I reiterated, "but she is an exception. This is Catherine. She's my girlfriend, and she's JD's mom."

"I'm what?" She turned to me now, that same look of disgust directed at me. "The only way I'm your girlfriend is that I'm a girl and I'm your friend, but one of those might no longer be the case."

"She's joining the dark side!" Allen announced. "The musky, brooding, dark underworld of masculinity. Please, join us!" He was dancing now, but soon slowed and then stopped. "Well, I think you two have some discussing to do."

Catherine found the red leather jacket and used it to line the wheelbarrow. She carefully placed six-year-old JD in there, as if it were still a few days ago, and then stalked out of the cabin as I chased behind.

She had already crossed my backyard when I caught up and grabbed her wrist. I pulled her arm around, and she used the momentum to turn and slap me. A warm prickle shot through my neck and bled into my face. I was stung, completely shocked, and unsure of who I was looking at. I held my cheek in my hand and stepped back. My throat closed and tears welled up, but I did everything I could to hold them back.

"You...you *hit* me."

"This is wrong, Noah, and you've dragged me into this."

I recognized the puzzled expression on her face; it was the same one she wore to pore over difficult exam questions at school. She looked ashamed for hitting me, but also justified in her decision.

"You need to tell your parents today, or else I'm not talking to you again. If you won't do anything to fix it, I don't want to have any part in this." She gestured between us.

"Catherine." I was still holding my cheek. "You're my only friend. I can't lose you. I can't just abandon them. What do you want me to do?"

"You didn't have to bring them back to life. You know what I want you to do." She was standing with both her hands on her hips.

"But Catherine," I said, struggling to find the right answer, the one that would let me keep them both. "*You're tearing me apart.*"

I had seen Catherine upset, disgusted, and angered, but I hadn't seen what Catherine looked like when someone let her down. "Goodbye, Noah." I watched her turn and walk away, not knowing then that it would be the last time we'd speak.

Catherine. Catherine in your cut-off shorts. Catherine with your crustless sandwiches. I should have chosen you.

Corey had a similar reaction to Catherine when I finally showed him. He didn't have much of a care for *how*—he jumped right to what was to come. It was the first weekend he visited, and I asked him to go on a walk. We snuck around the side of the house. Inside the shed, once the shock subsided, Corey recited a few of Allen's poems to him that he had memorized, and the two danced and held hands. James sat on the workbench clapping. He was about thirteen by then and quite skinny, but had skipped any awkward, gawky stages.

A plan was hatched. When Corey was heading back home later that night, he would drive around the corner and wait at the stop sign. Five minutes later, Allen would take JD and sneak through the cedars, then jump in the back seat and live with Corey at his new apartment. We resolved that I would visit on the weekends and after school when I could.

Corey rented a small studio with the help of my parents, and he would let them live there so long as they eventually found a way to pitch in on rent. That way he would no longer need help from his parents, relinquishing another yoke—a chain that yanked him back home. I think he would have let them stay for free. They could smoke, drink tea, and discuss Allen's and James' work.

That first week I visited every day after school, telling my parents I was going to a friend's house. My parents were thrilled I had come out of my shell and become so social, but they were also nervous it might eventually peter out, so they thought it best to proceed with caution and not ask too many questions. They always smiled enthusiastically and watched me bike off to the bus stop.

On the weekends, the four of us watched all of JD's movies, and then we watched them again and acted them out. Allen read his poetry to us, and we wandered through the city, covering Allen and JD in baggy hoodies, coiling scarfs around their faces. We climbed Mount Royal and howled at the moon. Neither Allen nor James seemed displeased with our arrangement, but I knew they couldn't live in Corey's apartment forever. But I didn't think about that much. I had everything I wanted, and I didn't want to think about what would come next.

James and Allen found a way to live in this world. They busked on the streets in sunglasses, baseball caps, and large coats. They looked scruffy and people mistook them for homeless, and though they got the occasional double-take, no one ever stopped to ask any further. On occasion, they got told that they looked like themselves. It all worked well for a couple of years, and they were my best friends, Corey too. Even when Corey lived at home, we had never spent this much time together. The three of them shaped me and taught me almost everything I knew.

The Monday after I had introduced Allen to Catherine, her locker was empty. There were no new students, so no one came to replace her. It was empty for the rest of that first year of high school. Whenever I saw her, she never looked at me. She had found a group of friends through Drama Club. I sat alone at our old table and watched from across the cafeteria as she slowly seemed to forget about me entirely. I tried once to approach her and apologize, but as I walked toward her, she looked at me. It was the first time she had looked at me since it all happened. She looked so sad, so disappointed. I decided to turn and walk away.

The last I heard, James and Allen were living in Vegas performing as look-alikes. They were making a killing, living in high-rise lofts, gambling their fortunes, and never thining to question their second chance at life. They had already lived their first lives as if they were second chances. Their riches and successes in Sin City were relayed to me by Corey, who kept in touch by postcard, and occasionally visited.

James had continued to age a year a day until he

stopped aging at twenty-four, which was how old he was when he had died. As James moved through childhood and adolescence, he began to remember who he was. This was expedited by a homeschooled education involving screenings of his own films. Allen Ginsberg never aged. I'm not sure he ever knew he had left and come back again.

The last time I saw James and Allen was in Corey's studio. I was in university by then, nineteen years old and studying English literature, just like Corey. I skipped one of my afternoon classes and climbed into his studio through the fire escape. JD, Allen, and Corey were all sitting on two couches they had dragged in from a dumpster. They were smoking weed with wet tea bags on their eyes, a couple of empty bottles of wine already on the table in font of them.

"We studied you in one of my poetry seminars, Allen." I broke the mellowed silence, trudging through the garbage everywhere. The place was disgusting. None of them ever cleaned. I sat down and joined them. Allen didn't remove the tea bags from his eyes, or his head from the pillow that propped up his neck.

"Don't listen to a word they say," he said, smiling. "Academics don't know anything about my writing."

"We troubled your work and your life. My professor said he knew you, that he met you once. That you had a reputation."

"Like I said—" He lifted one tea bag, and flashed a

grin that showed his gums and all his teeth. "They don't know a thing."

James was asleep and Corey was nodding to some imperceptible music. I was frustrated with them all, for how they had been living, for not seeming to notice that we had been growing apart.

"Allen, I'm not sure you're a good influence."

The joint was in my hand now, and I smoked the rest of it right down to the filter. The ember burned my fingers.

"You're a big boy, Noah. You can make your own choices. You don't have to listen to what people tell you. Haven't I told you that already?" He removed his tea bag once more to look for the joint and sulked when he saw it was done.

That might have been the problem. I was making my own choices. I was growing up, and all the while Allen and James remained the same.

"You know I'm going on a semester abroad in the winter," I said.

"Is that right?"

I had told Allen this three times already. It was fall, and the semester was over in a couple of weeks. Soon it would be Christmas, which Allen didn't celebrate, and then I'd be gone for six months.

"Well, you know Uncle Al will miss you. By the way, James, Corey, and I have been talking about some travels too. We were talking about inviting you, but you've got your school and all."

He had mentioned it half a dozen times, but they

had never bothered to ask. I wasn't sure they'd invite me if I wasn't in school. They spent most of their time busking and sitting in that studio together. I had been spending less and less time with them.

"You know you guys never thanked me."

"For what?" Allen got up and grabbed his coat from the upright coat hanger.

"Bringing you back."

"Did you do that?" He genuinely look perplexed, like this was the first time he had thought of it.

"Never mind."

"Do you remember Catherine?" I asked.

"Is she the one that keeps spending the night with Corey?"

"No, she visited the shed once, back when you lived there."

"Right…no recollection, sorry. I'm off on a hash run. I'll see you when I see you, Jimbo."

I was tired, and as I watched Allen gather some belongings from a cot and tie them in a little blanket attached to a stick, I fought against the heavy weight, the drooping of my eyelids. *It's time for me to leave*, I thought as I was drifting off. I thought about Catherine. I thought about Catherine's face. It's what I thought of as I watched Allen climb the ledge and leave from the window. He turned the corner and disappeared into the afternoon through the fire escape.

Hundred-Year Flood Line

When I invited Don to stay for dinner, something in his face changed. But I only thought of that the next day.

"If it isn't a bother," he said.

"Not at all. I was making extra portions anyway."

He passed behind me through the kitchen as I sliced cloves of garlic for the Tagliatelle Bolognese. The kitchen lights were dimmed and the satellite radio played old songs from the backyard. He closed the sliding glass door behind him as the music phased out to a muffled bass, and sank into the patio chair next to my mother for another glass of wine.

A bloated Frost Moon hung by a cord in the sky and reflected off the surface of Lac des Deux Montagnes behind them. Don had taught me that each month had a unique name for its respective moon. November's full moon was the Beaver Moon, but it was also called the Frost Moon in Cree and the Freezing Moon by the Anishinaabe. Donald had sailed his whole life, and he knew these things. He knew about the moons, the winds, and the waters. He had taken me sailing a few times and taught me how to read a wind vane atop a mast, and that white caps tend to crest when the wind is blowing at roughly ten knots. Since my parents' divorce, Don had been spending a lot of time with my mom, and I had been visiting and spending more time with both of them. They had met in their photography club. My dad had been unfaithful for years. I was glad she was letting someone in.

I salted the pasta water and stirred the boiling pot with a wooden spoon before pouring in the tagliatelle, then watched the noodles get sucked into the whirlpool. They bobbed back to the surface.

Behind me, the door slid open. Don poked his head in, smiling. "You know, I have to say, watching you cook is an absolute treat, Seymour. Your mom and I have been observing through the window—so concentrated, so passionate. It's a joy to see."

"Thanks, Don."

He went back outside as quick as he had snuck in.

The sun was setting, though it was only 5 p.m. The clocks had just turned back an hour, and winter was encroaching. When the sub-zero temperatures came in a few weeks, the lake would begin to freeze over and the snow would reflect the moonlight, and it would no longer get so dark. The Frost Moon would become the December Cold Moon, and Don would retire his kayak for the winter season and cross-country ski across the lake. Don said kayaking this late in the season was his favourite part of the year, when he had the lake all to himself. He lived on the other side of Lac des Deux Montagnes, in Vaudreuil, and it was only a fifteen-minute paddle from our house in Sainte-Anne-de-Bellevue.

My mom came back in and placed two glasses next to the sink. "Don had to leave. He told me to tell you that he says goodbye."

"He was supposed to stay for dinner."

"I know. He told me you invited him. That was nice. It makes him happy, you know. I think he was guilty he had to leave."

She looked tired, and so did the skin on her arms. The muscles were slowly letting go of the bones. But she was smiling, and despite being tired I could see that she was happy again. It was her eyes, how she could look directly into mine. It had been six or seven years since my mom finally left my dad, and until Don there hadn't been a man around. I vaguely knew she was going out on some dates, but they never came to anything. When I asked, she'd say *Men are the worst* or *I'd rather be alone.* There was also the man in the grocery store who grabbed her ass when she was bending over to pick up a bag of milk. She planted her foot and swung the bag of milk around, putting her full weight into it. The bag exploded on his chest and he fell back into a shelf of canned soup. I remembered thinking that life must be harder for women.

"Why'd he go?"

"He said he had some work to take care of tonight,

and if he stayed for dinner then he would stay for the rest of the bottle of wine, too."

"Well, goodbye, Don." I waved out at the lake, my reflection waving back in the glass door.

She picked up the bottle of Barolo they had been drinking and took out two new glasses. She held the bottle up to me, as if asking a question, and I nodded. The dish I'd prepared was a new recipe for me, and so the ceremony was to sit down and praise how good it was as we ate it. The praise wasn't elaborate, only the occasional *delicious* or *oh my God,* and even those slowly became gratified noises, *mmmmm* or *mhm.* Then with bellies full and an openness to critique alongside a fresh glass of wine, we would discuss how it could be better.

"It was delicious, but I think the ratio of noodles to sauce was off."

"You're right, I'll have to stir in fewer noodles next time."

"Or more sauce."

"Right, or more sauce. That too."

"Or fewer noodles *and* more sauce," she said.

"Too far, Mom."

We gathered all the dishes and let them pile up by the sink, a mess to be cleaned up in the morning. We drank our wine, laughed, played a few games of backgammon, tallied the ongoing score in our tournament, and noted that my mom was still ahead. The room felt full and yet it felt like someone was missing. I had a Sunday Zoom

meeting the next morning, so I went to bed early.
The lake was as calm as it ever was in November, but spring was a different story. Floods in Sainte-Anne-de-Bellevue had been getting worse the past three years, with each spring surpassing the hundred-year flood line and the damage caused by the previous spring's floods. The hundred-year flood line demarcated the zones on the flood map where there was a one-percent chance of a flood happening in any given year. As maps were being updated and property values were plummeting, people around us were selling their waterfront homes.

It felt like the whole island of Montreal would be submerged in a couple of years. Every local news channel broadcasted the same images from across the West Island: people canoeing down main boulevards in Pierrefonds, flooded grocery stores and schools, elderly couples evacuated from their condo balconies by helicopter, silhouettes hanging by a cord suspended in the air. Politicians posed with Billy boots and sandbags in Pointe-Claire Village on these same news channels, thumbs pointed God-ward, demonstrating the Great Collective Effort and their support for the community, while all around them the Coast Guard evacuated people from their homes.

My father came to help with the house the spring after he left, before Don was around. He didn't usually come around the house anymore, but Mom had pulled a muscle in her back during a dragon-boating tournament and preparing for the floods was more than a one-person job. While Mom stayed in her room and avoided my father, we installed new sump pumps in the crawlspace below our home and built a barricade of sandbags all around our property.

Mom and Dad didn't talk any more than they needed to—they had demarcated their own line, and it was never to be crossed. The city dropped off pallets of sandbags along the streets, and after a long winter, it was astonishing to watch all our neighbours pouring out of their homes, their families and friends driving down to help out, everyone offering a hand where they could. Helicopters carrying news reporters flew above our homes, and from above I couldn't help but think that we must have looked like a colony of ants.

Dad didn't think much of the hundred-year flood line. "Most people don't even have a good grasp of statistics," I remember him saying last spring. "The hundred-year flood zone doesn't mean much." He wiped the sweat from his brow with his forearm. "It could be due to the dams opening upstream in Ontario."

I followed behind him, arms hanging, fully extended, barely propping up a bag of sand. I wore gardening gloves that I'm not convinced helped at all. "Three years in a row. You don't think that means anything?"

City workers in orange hi-vis vests drove in on city trucks, asking where their help was needed.

"It could, but weather patterns fluctuate. So it could also not."

As we lugged sandbags from the pallets to the house, I suggested that the odds of flooding within the hundred-year zone for three consecutive years were astronomically low, and he dismissed it all.

"Actually, I have news." He dropped the sandbag onto the pile and stood with his hands on his hips, breathing heavy. "I'm using this as an opportunity. I'm moving out of the condo I've been renting and into a waterfront home I bought a few roads down. I couldn't help it. Property's a steal these days. I'll be moving in with Keeley so we can all spend more time together."

His breathing steadied as he delivered this news. I stood quietly and didn't say anything, mostly stunned. I wasn't sure if I was more upset about his lack of concern about the floods, his buying a home on the water, or his buying a home so close to Mom. I told him that was great, even though I couldn't think of anything more selfish.

Keeley pulled up in a Mercedes SUV just as we finished. She was wearing a furry pink Adidas tracksuit and large round sunglasses that covered most of her face. She rolled down the window and waved enthusiastically. I lifted my hand and forced a smile.

"Well," I said, "thanks for the help with this, Dad."

"Sure thing. You should join us for dinner tonight."

"I'll think about it," I said, with no intention of going.

We hugged and he got in the car. Keeley had covered the passenger seat in black garbage bags. He accidentally lifted one of the bags with him as he climbed in and sat on the tan leather seat beneath. She smacked his shoulder, and then waved goodbye. "You should join us for dinner," she shouted out the window.

"Thinking about it!" I gave her a thumbs up.

My parents had each been vacationing during the first of the three floods. My father and Keeley were in Myrtle Beach, South Carolina, which is where she was from, and my mom was in Tremblant with her girlfriends. While they were away, my uncle came to help me stack sandbags, and I slept on the couch in the living room every night so I could hear the alarms in the crawlspace if our sump pumps stopped working. I resented that my dad was on a beach in the place where he had met Keeley on a business trip while still with married to my mom—voluntarily swimming in water—while I was sleeping on a couch and sore from the day's labour. *Sometimes, you have to be selfish in life,* he once told me. I knew it was immature, but I secretly blamed the floods on him, and everyone like him.

One night the alarms in the crawlspace went off and my eyes shot open. There was a weight on my chest preventing me from sitting up. I couldn't move at all; my limbs wouldn't respond. The living room filled with water pouring in through the windows. I felt the cold crawling up the side of my face, an animal panic surging in my throat, and then I was completely submerged and watching air bubbles rising up from my mouth. I woke up in a panicked sweat to a quiet, dry room.

We never heard helicopters whirring outside at 3 a.m. in November, cutting through the sky like overfed dragonflies, but that's what happened that night Don left before my tagliatelle. I stared up at the dark ceiling, unsure if it was another dream or reality. It wasn't the sump pumps, I thought, so it wasn't my problem. The helicopters mingled into the morning as I dozed in and out of sleep, wondering if there had been a duck-hunting accident in one of the hunting blinds.

I went downstairs and turned the light on to make a coffee. Mom was already sitting at the table in a baggy white T-shirt, dark circles under her eyes from lack of sleep. Mornings, I'd usually find her watching the news in her bedroom; I'd walk by, wave to her, make a coffee downstairs, then come back up to my bedroom to get ready for work. This morning, she was still sitting where I had last seen her. She tried to say something, but her voice cracked. She placed her hands on the table.

The kayak had been found downstream, but there was still no body.

My stomach rose into my chest, and a wave of possible scenarios flashed through my mind. I knew this routine; I knew that voice. I had seen death and loss before, and it was often news that came from my mother. Her cell rang and she picked it up.

"I have to go down to the college," she said. "They found him by the shore." She looked whiter still, animal-like. I helped her up by the elbow, and she looked around, though her eyes didn't focus on anything. She walked by me, and passed through the back door. I offered to drive, but she insisted on going alone.

I sat down at the table and remembered Don's face. His expression, how it changed. *Why had his face changed when I asked him to stay for dinner? Did he know something?* The memory of it rose from my chest, like it had been buried there, waiting to be remembered. I searched it for meaning, looking for something I might have missed that, had it been noticed, could have helped prevent this from happening. But there was nothing to look for, nothing to change.

Don and I had been getting closer. I never saw him as someone who wanted to replace our father, or who lessened the chances of my parents getting back together. As far as I was concerned, those chances were lower than the chances of the river surpassing the hundred-year flood line. I only ever saw him as someone who cared about my mom, and that's all I wanted for her. She deserved that.

I liked spending time with them, if only to see her happy with someone. We did things together, too. Don and my mom both loved the water. My mom was an avid paddler herself. We'd go for evening paddles together, sometimes with a cigar, and watch the sun set. One trip, we paddled past my dad's house. I had already known about it, but wasn't sure what my mom knew. As we paddled by, the sun was setting and all the lights in the waterfront homes were switched on. I squinted and peered into my dad's new house, and saw him and Keeley slow-dancing in the living room. I looked to my mom and Don, both enamoured with the newly unveiled stars in the sky. I didn't look back at the house, and suggested we go home.

On another night that summer, the three of us sat out on the Adirondack chairs in Mom's backyard, watching the ripples in the water disrupt the previously perfect full moon. My mom went to use the washroom. We had been drinking; I lost count of how many, maybe four or five beers each. In a slipped confession, I admitted that I had always wanted to learn to sail. Don looked at me and began laughing. I bowed my head, a little ashamed. He told me that he had been sailing his whole life, was certified, and had even taught a bunch of courses. He said he would teach me, that he could take me out on the water next week. *A good sailor lives and dies by the water*, he said. At the time, I thought this was something to laugh at, and so I did.

My mom came back outside and sat on the grass between our chairs. The moon reflected off her, too, and her hair looked like silk. She smiled, and asked what we had been talking about. Don grinned my way, knowingly. I mirrored his smile. "Nothing," we said. "Nothing much at all."

I got the details in short bursts throughout the rest of the day, word of mouth travelling through phone calls and Facebook groups faster than local news coverage. Concerned citizens had been posting on a West Island Facebook group about a missing fifty-six-year-old man. An older photo of him circulated around the Internet, in which he looked much younger than I'd ever seen him. I recalled my reflection waving back to me in the glass door the night before.

Don's friends came over in groups, gathering on the patio, wanting to be near the last place he'd been, to feel what was left of him. They looked out over the water and cried. Everyone knew that accidents happen, but no one could understand this one. He knew the waters, which spots to avoid. Some brought bagels, others brought lemon cake. I served teas and whiskeys, bussing empty glassware and dirty dishes, catching snippets of conversation between taxied trips from the patio and the kitchen.

...He wasn't breathing when they found him...

"Cream or sugar, Darlene?" I asked.

...People reported hearing several cries for help near the rapids, so they called the police...

"Whiskey with that, Scott? Let me take that from you." I took his empty glass.

...He was drinking wine the night it happened. Do you think he was drunk?

"I don't know what to say..." I said.

...The water levels have been rising. I think it's the fault of the floods. The newer water levels create new

rapids. Those Vaudreuil rapids were already vicious.

"It's been so long since I've seen you, Tina." I hugged her. "Thank you for coming."

...The fireman on site told us that there was still hope, that sometimes the hypothermia preserves the body after cardiac arrest.

Eventually I brought out some extra lawn chairs and everyone sat in a circle, listening to the geese while waiting their turn to share stories.

One of Don's friends, Darlene, said. "The last funeral I attended was for a friend who was a motorcycle enthusiast. As the speeches were about to begin, a revving motorcycle engine filled the funeral home. Everyone looked around, confused. It seemed be playing from the building's PA system, but then it passed. The windows were open, so nobody talked about it, but everybody came to the same conclusion."

Looking up at the birds, Darlene said Don would come back, just like her other friend had during his funeral. Don always used to check up on her with random phone calls. "An annoying shit," she said. Everybody laughed. Some of us cried. Only my mom sat still, breathing carefully, taking time to fill her lungs.

The image of his bloated body floating down the current stayed with me. Whether I smiled or laughed, I couldn't get it out of my head. All that was left was that image. He must have been so cold. What was he thinking about before he lost consciousness? He floated in my head, then dipped underwater. I waited for him to come back up for air, gasping.

I went inside to do dishes and watched everyone through the window, my hands covered in suds. Cleaning up after others was the only thing I could manage to do. The thought of Mom losing this special person weighed on me. I imagined her having to go on dates again, with men who complimented her eyes and grabbed her ass. I pictured her in an empty kitchen, while my dad was in a warmly lit house a few streets down, dancing in the kitchen with Keeley, as outside the waterline quietly crept up.

Quietly, Loving Everyone

After dinner, Lenny and Izzy shared a cigarette on the balcony. It had been snowing all night and so they stood with one foot on the balcony and one in the living room, half in and half out, leaning against the door frame and blowing smoke toward the clouds. They shared old stories, laughter, and the same pair of shoes. The world was distant, and the snow kept everything at bay. The trees moved slowly in the wind. Billie Holiday sang sad melodies to an empty living room. In the bedroom over, next to Izzy's bookshelf, a two-day-old helium balloon drifted, slowly petering out.

They hadn't bothered to clear the table, instead basking in the aftermath of the gluttonous meal. The lamb shanks had been gnawed to the bone, fat floated like air bubbles on a sea of oil, and their plates still lay on a wooden crate beside an empty bottle of wine. They knew it would have to be cleaned up, but not right then.

Lenny's and Izzy's imprints, softly pressed into the carpet, were still visible on either side of the crate. They smoked the rest of their cigarette, coughing and laughing behind a glowing ember, and then lit a second from the remnants of the first.

The balloon was from Geoff's send-off party before his conference in Turkey. Izzy had been dating Geoff for two years and had moved into his apartment. Lenny had never met Geoff, but had observed evidence of him in the apartment—framed pictures of the couple, a stick of Old Spice deodorant in the bathroom, a man's belt hanging from the closet door.

"How's New York?" Izzy asked.

"Full of pigeons," Lenny said.

"Sounds like you were right to upend everything and rush down there. And the Master's program?"

"It's horrible, I'm kidding. I like the program too."

Lenny had left Montreal three years ago. At first he and Izzy had talked about trying long distance, but they were both in their early twenties at the time. They had things they still wanted to experience. Neither believed the long distance would work, so they got ahead of it and decided to end things on friendly terms instead of letting it sour over time. They had only been dating for a year, and before that they had been friends for a couple of years. One of them was always dating someone else. Once Izzy and Lenny started dating, they admitted they had always had a feeling that they would end up together. Their significant others probably sensed this, and it may have even led to some of those relationships ending. Even when they broke up, they agreed that they would probably still end up together again, after they had each lived more of their respective lives.

"And the acting?" he asked.

"Not paying the bills." She stole the smoke from Lenny's hands. "Still working at Café Myriade and doing some freelance design work on the side. Geoff doesn't charge me rent, which helps."

Lenny winced. "Any good roles?"

"I've been cast as Mimi in *La Bohème*. It'll be debuting at the Centaur in the spring."

"Why didn't you tell me?"

"Was I supposed to?"

"I'm sorry. I meant 'Congratulations.'" Lenny stole the cigarette back. "What's it about?"

"A bohemian seamstress and her entourage of socialites living in 1830s Paris."

"So not much acting involved?"

"You're an asshole."

During the winter and summer breaks, Lenny came back to Montreal to visit his mom, his friends, and Izzy. He didn't want to admit the latter to her. The first year, they were both single so they saw no problem hooking up. When Izzy started dating Geoff, they said they'd go back to being just friends, but they still hadn't managed.

"Don't take this the wrong way," he said. "I know you can sing, but *opera?*"

"Didn't you know?" Izzy held her arms out. "I'm a tour de force."

They stood in silence for a while. Lenny thought about their first cigarette, the first time they slept together, the first time she had asked him to tie her up, and that one time he drove her to the hospital after she fell off a swing and broke her nose. They finished the cigarette and went back in, sliding the door behind them and carrying the dishes to the kitchen sink.

It was December 27, the no man's land between Christmas and New Year's Eve. Lenny had texted Izzy. *Want to see me?* He had already spent too much time with his family. His friends were busy until New Year's Eve, and he missed her. To his surprise, she invited him over for dinner. She had never invited him over to the apartment because of Geoff. It felt risky, like they were crossing a line. They both knew they'd have to stop seeing each other soon, but not now. *One condition. Bring your mom's homemade Nanaimo bars*, she'd texted. *I know she always keeps a stash in the back of the fridge.*

Lenny rolled his sleeves up and poured some water into the sink. Izzy's reflection doubled in the kitchen window. With the chandelier on, it became a one-way mirror.

"I heard my neighbour crying last night," Izzy said into the cabinet where she kept the gin.

"What do you think they were crying about?"

"You tell me."

She pulled the ice tray from the freezer and bent the hard plastic over the counter until a few cubes popped out. Apart from the gin, she poured two other liquors he didn't recognize into their glasses.

"He's an older man who lives alone. No one visits him." She handed him a glass as he wiped the suds off on his shirt. "It's a Negroni. Sip it slowly."

She slouched down on the floor beside him, resting against the cabinets.

"Did you know your neighbours growing up?" she asked, sitting with her chest pressed against her knees.

"What did you say was in here? It's bitter as hell."

"I once helped him bring his groceries up. He invited me in for tea afterwards. I told him I had work. I still regret not going in. He's sweet and harmless."

"Do you have any soda I could dilute this with?"

Lenny placed the drink next to the edge of the sink, hoping it might fall in. He had neglected to mention that he had been seeing his neighbour Holly back in Brooklyn. He picked the drink back up and glanced around for something he could sweeten it with.

"Oh!" Izzy hopped back up and peeled a sliver of rind off an orange. She twirled the pith and pinched it toward Lenny, shooting a mist of citrus at him, then dropped it into his drink. "There," she said, and plopped back onto the floor. Once the dishes were done, they went over to the bedroom.

Lenny placed his drink on the nightstand and dove onto the bed. He pulled his phone from his pocket and played "Helplessness Blues" by Fleet Foxes, but it was still connected to the Bluetooth speaker in the next room over. There were three unopened texts from Holly. A surge ran through his body, followed by a pang of guilt. The thought of Geoff texting Izzy right now made him more bitter than his drink.

He wasn't technically cheating. He had met Holly in the program, and later found out they weren't only living in the same building but were neighbours. When they started regularly hooking up, he asked about their status. *I don't believe in monogamy,* Holly said. *I need to be able to love everyone.* Some nights of the week, through the thin walls, Lenny learned this was true.

But then again, he was cheating with Izzy. They were both cheating, together. He convinced himself that she might still love him and somehow it made his life more interesting, which he knew was selfish, but he also knew he loved her. He felt like he was less to blame. Any way he spun it, he would regret whichever relationship was undone.

Izzy splayed herself across the carpet, running her hands through the white fibres and her own black haloes of hair.

"When I was young," Lenny said, "my parents used to listen to our neighbours' conversations through my baby monitor."

"They spied on them?" Izzy asked.

"It wasn't the McCarthy era. Their voices came through and they'd just listen." He reluctantly finished his drink, wanting the effect more than the drink itself.

"Give it to me, I'll pour another round. Something different this time."

Lenny spoke up so Izzy could hear him from the kitchen. "They'd set up these baby monitors, you know, to check if I was breathing or something. And they'd be in the kitchen eating, and they'd hear these voices in the apartment."

"Mhmm."

"And they were just talking casually, like we are right now, you know? Just these voices. Two people talking, clear as day."

Izzy came back with two glasses of wine. She handed one over and sat next to him on the bed, her feet dangling off the edge. Lenny hopped off and paced the room.

"My mom and dad decided to open a bottle of wine and just sit there, listening. They made a game of it. They'd invent different contexts each time, but it was always the same couple. Other times, they'd listen for a bit and then turn off the speaker and ad-lib the rest of the conversation."

Lenny put his drink down and lay on the floor, his head resting on the carpet. He noticed the cracked plaster on the ceiling and wondered what would leak through if it cracked any further.

"Mom used to tell me these stories after Dad left. It was our way of reminiscing. I was young, but after he left, it's like we had been woken from a dream."

"Did they hear anything good?"

"The couple spent a few weeks planning a heist."

"You're kidding?" Izzy sat up. "Did they do it?"

"That's not what's important."

Izzy fell back on top of the comforter.

"Some nights, the couple fought over whose turn it was to take out the trash. Others, they planned a heist. They read to their child before bed. They watched porn. They role-played. '*Please, take anything you find, just don't hurt me or my child … No, not the lamp! That belonged to my great aunt Mary! Seriously … Steve. Steve. Watch the lamp.*'"

Izzy and Lenny both laughed, and like most good laughs, they felt the silence in the room when it was over.

"It's strange to think of these things happening around us," Izzy said. "I wonder what people would think if they listened to us."

Lenny stared at the ceiling and closed his eyes and tried to listen to the lives playing out around them. When he opened his eyes and looked over at her, there she was sitting on the edge of her bed with her toes running through the carpet next to his face, looking back at him. There she was. He thought about the dinner they had made, and about when it had gotten complicated. He heard somebody coughing behind the walls, as if they were being listened to. She must have heard it too.

"We can't keep doing this," Izzy finally said.

"Geoff… You're happy with him?" Lenny asked.

"I'm with him, Lenny. He's nice to me. He knows what he wants."

The walls felt like they were leaning in. Things might have been different if he'd asked her to go with him to New York, or if he had stayed. Lenny's phone vibrated in his pocket, which felt like Holly's hand rubbing his thigh.

"He's going to propose when he comes back."

"How do you know?"

"Two years is a long time, Lenny. The world doesn't stop just because you want things to be as they were when you left them. He's older. He's got different priorities and a career, he wants different things out of life than you do."

"How do you know what I want?"

"I don't. I'm not sure you do either."

"What if I said I'd leave New York tomorrow to come back?" Lenny asked.

"It's not the same as doing it."

"So now what?"

Though Izzy's face was blank, behind it a thousand decisions had likely already been made. She went to the kitchen and came back with the bottle of gin. She tried to smile as she handed him the bottle. Earlier, he had been thinking about some of their firsts, and now he thought about all of their lasts.

"Come here," she said.

Sitting on a stool and rubbing cream on her face after, Izzy studied Lenny through the vanity mirror. He lay naked atop her unmade bed, tearing matches from a matchbook and tossing them at the balloon.

"I hate you now," Izzy announced. "You can't just come in and out of people's lives."

"Actually, you can. People do it all the time."

Izzy held Lenny's gaze through the mirror and twisted the bottom of a lipstick tube. "I don't want you to spend the night."

Lenny didn't move from the bed. Soon, she joined him and, with her head on his chest, they fell asleep. He woke up to the sound of his phone vibrating. It had fallen from his pocket as they frantically undressed and was now buzzing along the floor, the screen lighting up the room. A fleet of snow removal trucks drove by. The floorboards shuddered beneath the bed. He got the panicky feeling that the whole world wanted in on their room, and he didn't want to let them in. He heard footsteps climbing the stairs and knew that if the door handle jiggled, and the door opened, it would all be over sooner than he was ready for.

Izzy was breathing beside him. He saw her face in the phone screen's light; her eyes were wide open, staring up at the ceiling. He knew the whole world would implode on them one day.

"It makes me sad to think about it," she whispered into the dark.

"What does?" Lenny asked.

"To hear his footsteps going up those stairs."

Lenny listened but heard only the sirens outside.

"Why is that so sad?"

"Because he's going to the same room he always does, to the same couch, to watch the same TV."

"So?" he asked.

"How's it any different than a coffin?"

He thought about it for a while, about all the rooms along the street. Maybe they were all coffins. He wondered what Izzy thought it meant to be alive. Of course, the man could get up and leave his room at any point, and so it was quite different.

"I think we should try and get some sleep." He threw the covers over her head; she pulled them back down and got up. Lenny tried to listen for a TV through the walls. There was nothing but the sound of the fridge and the clock ticking on the wall. He thought about all the people living and dying in their rooms and wondered how many of them thought about it that way.

She turned on the upright lamp in the corner of her bedroom, then scanned the bookshelf next to it. The balloon drifted in front of the books and as Izzy swatted it, it finally popped. She jumped backward and laughed in relief. Izzy removed a book of poetry from the shelf. "Do you remember that poetry class we took in CEGEP?"

"The one with the Russian professor."

"That's it, and how he always used to go on these incredible tangents about life and death."

"You used to do such a good impersonation of him."

Izzy grinned, placing the opened anthology on her head as if to fashion a traditional ushanka hat. She began speaking in an accent, pacing the room.

"*But of course, the only medicine for the agony of being is love.*" She gestured with her hands, pointing at something imperceptible, then pretended to comb her fingers through her beard. "*And of course, you just need to sit down and write it, you know. Anywhere. On a napkin, a brown paper bag, a leaf, a fogged-up mirror. You need to be madly in love, with anything, with anyone, so much so that you can't keep it in.*"

Lenny applauded her performance as she bowed. The book fell from her head and onto the wooden floor.

"Do you want me to read one to you?"

"Only if you do it in that accent."

She picked it up and fanned through the book, randomly placing a finger on the now-stopped page.

"'My Husband Discovers Poetry,' by Diane Lockward."

She sat back down and began to read. Halfway through the poem, she stopped reading and closed the book. She didn't look up right away, just sat there with her head hung, and after a while he noticed she was shaking. Lenny didn't get up. He knew that if he got up to touch her, it would only make things worse.

"Do you think we can love more than one person at once?" she finally asked from behind her hands.

"Sure, yeah. In different ways, maybe."

"Do you believe that?"

"It depends on what you mean by *love*," Lenny said. "But really, I'm not so sure."

"I don't think so either."

His phone buzzed again. The trucks removed snow from the streets outside while a whole city slept behind closed doors and thin walls. He felt like picking up the phone, but not right then as they quietly—so as not to reveal anything to the neighbours—listened to the humming and dying of it all.

"Come back to bed, Izzy. We'll figure it out in the morning."

She sat in her chair a while longer, contemplating the room as it orbited around her. When she stood up, she turned the upright lamp off, taking her time to feel her way through the dark. There were no more balloons left to pop. The party was over.

"Would you tell me that story about the baby monitors again?" Izzy asked.

Lenny began telling the story once more, but before he finished, he felt her breath slow and then steady next to him. Her breathing, that peaceful surrender, made him wonder if maybe things could be different in the morning. Outside that window, beyond the snow trucks, the world was always changing. People were experimenting, opening their lives and their love. It was too late for some things, but other things would stick around for a while longer. He didn't know what to believe. Soon he would fall asleep, but first he wanted to lie next to her a while longer, listening to her quiet breath.

We Should Change the Curtains

"WE SHOULD CHANGE the curtains."

It had been a while since either of them had spoken. Joy couldn't remember what he had last said. She watched the dust rising through the light, doubled through her smoke, and took another drag.

"What's wrong with them?" she finally asked.

"They don't keep the water in," Joseph said.

She squinted, studying the living room drapes, then turned to take him in. He was smoking a cigarette while staring at a fixed spot on the wall, a great stillness glossed over his face, a synthetic unawareness, as if he had briefly stepped out of his corpse and left the room. She thought of those storefront mannequins. She wondered if he was thinking about the last time the water came in; she didn't know what that meant.

"You mean the condensation?"

"What?"

"The condensation," Joy said. "You mean they let the condensation in."

Joy nibbled the cracked coat of lime green polish that Viviane had painted onto her fingernails during her last visit over a month ago. She observed the spot he was studying where the wallpaper had begun to peel. It was between their piano and the portrait taken at their cabin on Lac Brome—the two of them standing in tall grass, holding Rose up by her hands. Cliff and the twins weren't born yet. It was just the three of them. She tried to remember when the photo was taken. They all looked so young. It was at least thirty years ago, so she placed it sometime in the early-seventies. Her hair hadn't yet greyed, and her husband's face had wrinkles but only in the good spots—the kinds that form around the eyes with too much sun and laughter, not between the eyebrows from a furrowed brow. She decided not to compare the image with the man sitting next to her; she lit a cigarette and decided it wasn't that long ago.

"I meant the shower curtain."

"I thought you meant those ones." She pointed at the window.

"Why? What's wrong with those?"

They looked like they might disintegrate if the wind blew through. They were the same ones that had come with the house a lifetime ago.

"Nothing," she said. "There's nothing wrong with them. I just thought that's what you meant."

"Right. Well, I think we should change the shower curtains."

He scratched at the scruff growing on his face, looking at the same spot on the wall, and they both wondered how long it had been.

"Why do they need to be changed?" she asked.

"I already told you. They don't keep the water in."

"Right," she said. "I'm sorry."

They sat in silence a while longer, hardly stirring, moving only their cigarettes closer to their mouths. They did this often, sitting in their living room while it rained, looking out past their backyard onto the highway and the tracks. They had arranged the room just for this design, so they could sit and smoke. They lined the room with family portraits—tiny windows into the absence that Rose, then the boys, then Viviane left behind—a brick mantel littered with piano recital trophies, yellow wallpaper printed with red swirls, and these two sun-worn leather chairs on either side of the futon they had bought in case any guests stayed the night. This didn't happen often. When it did, the room's stale odor was masked with Febreze.

"Do you listen?"

"What?"

"When I talk to you, do you listen?" he repeated, tapping on the armrest. "I always have to ask you something twice, and even then, when I ask you the same thing a week later, you've already forgotten."

"I'm sorry. I listen. We'll change the curtain." She didn't want to start another fight. "You just catch me lost in thought sometimes."

"Rose used to say the same, you know."

She had given up on trying to remember how Rose used to be. It still made her sad that they had lost her the way they did. Poor Viviane, never knowing her mother and then only finding out when she was gone. She focused instead on the possibility that she would have to buy a new shower curtain at the mall now, which made her uneasy. Walking by those storefront mannequins—how they stared at her with indifference as she passed—an uncanny reflection of God observing her own sadness. Were those mannequins manufactured in sets? Did they stay together beyond the season?

"I'll go to the store tomorrow. What do you want?"

"I don't know." He exhaled his smoke. "What do you think?"

"How about one of those old maps? The ones they used to have in college dorms."

"God no. That's a horrible idea," he said. "Aren't we a little old for that?"

"I'm sorry, you're right, we are. I was just thinking of those days. What do you think then?"

Joy stubbed her butt into an overflowing ashtray on the coffee table, then lit another cigarette and gazed at the piano. She thought of Rose's fingers when she did—slender fingers, stretching across the keys, tickling those ivory chords. They had paid for lessons when she was a child, and she played beautifully. She learned Bach's "Goldberg Variations" in her third year and began composing in her fourth. So much potential before getting pregnant so young. On rainy days, often early on Sunday mornings, her fingers overrode the sounds of the passing trains and cars rolling by, shutting out all the noise and all the rooms outside of that one. She imagined a whole world of people sitting and smoking, all looking out onto the tracks, all waiting for the train to pass them by.

She wondered if Rose would still be alive if they hadn't insisted on taking her daughter away from her. If Joseph hadn't been so consumed with how it would look: their daughter with a daughter of her own at that age, how it would have ruined her future. Would Rose still be playing the piano? Joy shifted her gaze to the window and watched the raindrops follow the rivulets of the ones that fell before them. They started slow when they landed, but picked up momentum the longer they rolled and the faster they fell. This was until, like all the others, they disappeared out of sight, gone over the edge.

"Maybe just a solid colour," he said. "Something that will match the accents. How about blue?"

She thought about it for a while.

"I don't think Viviane would like that. She'd call it square or something. How about polka dots?"

He took a drag, held it, and released it with a sigh. She had unsettled him. He pulled another cigarette out from the pack.

"So why do you ask," he said, "if you're going to reject all my suggestions?"

"I'm sorry. You're right. It's not a bad idea. I just don't think it's what Viviane would want."

"Well, she doesn't live here anymore, does she? And what about our boys, about what they want?"

She thought his question was accusatory, but didn't want to start another fight. "I know, but they don't visit as often, not that any of them do. But when she does come back, I want her to feel at home."

She was out of smokes and asked him for another. He gave her one.

"Well it is her home, and that's not dependent on the shower curtain, is it?"

"No, it isn't," she said.

"If she doesn't feel at home, for whatever reason, of all the possibilities, the shower curtain is the least of our concern, for God's sake."

She thought about that as she lit the cigarette: about her husband, about his stubborn preference for the sons who no longer visited him, about Rose and the humiliation he said she'd brought upon him twice—the second with getting pregnant, the first for being born by another man—about the way he still looked at Viviane like a problem that couldn't be solved, about the shower curtain they had bought years ago, about God's sake. She tried to remember when and where they had bought it, but she couldn't quite recall. In any case, the store was probably long gone.

Her thoughts trickled back into the room with the smell of smoke. Not cigarette smoke, but real smoke. Grey tendrils rose from a carpet-borne flame and were climbing up the leg of their coffee table. Joseph jumped up and swatted at it for a few seconds before smothering it with a blanket. By the time it was extinguished, he was sweating through his shirt. He looked over at his wife, who was no longer holding her cigarette.

"What the *hell was that* for?" He fell into his chair.

"Everything's always my fault, isn't it?"

"Well maybe it *is*," he said.

She sat up in her chair and stiffened her neck. "Don't talk to me like that. Don't you dare. You're bitter."

"And why do you think that is?" Joseph asked.

"I know why. You as good as sulk whenever you're around me. You don't think I've tried hard enough since her death. You feel like you lost us both, that I don't pay enough attention to you or our boys."

"She was my daughter too—I took you both in."

"You *see*! You say that like it's a charity act!"

The whole room felt like brittle kindling. She tried looking at something else in the room, anything but the leather chair next to her and the man sitting in it. Now she'd have to buy another carpet, too. She sat there, stunned, angry with him and all the shower curtains of this world that let out water. Her eye landed on the piano, and she let herself drift off again.

The first time she had tried playing that piano was with Rose. A moka pot had been percolating on the stovetop the morning the softest sounds she had ever heard trickled into the kitchen from the living room. She stood there for a moment, wondering where it was coming from. She wondered how her own daughter, this strange little angel, could just sit down at the piano and decipher it like that. A coffee mug in hand, she floated into the next room, where her entrance went unnoticed as Rose's brown curls bobbed over the piano. When she finished, she turned around and smiled.

"Hi, Mommy."

"When did you learn that, sweetheart?"

"This morning, while you and Joseph were sleeping."

Not a note of vanity in her voice. She was still young enough to be unaware. Joy wished she would start calling him "Dad."

"I wish I could play."

"Don't be silly, Mom. I'll show you."

She sat on the bench next to Rose, who began playing once more, her fingers darting across the keys.

"I could never play anything like that."

Rose improvised a waltz riff over the melody of "Chopsticks." Rose was sitting right next to her, but she already felt out of reach.

As Joy leaned over to kiss her daughter on the cheek, she filtered back into the room and tried to remember where she was. She looked between the rain and the picture on the wall, then back again to the cars passing and the trains rolling by, and finally at the man sitting next to her. He sat still, staring out the window. She thought about it all, about the curtain that might have had polka dots, about Rose, about why they kept the piano if no one really played. She tried not to care about the polka dots or the number of years.

It had been a while since either of them spoke. She couldn't remember what she had last said. She looked at the curtains and the world setting behind them—both filtered through that room—and took another drag.

"Blue," she finally said. "Blue should be fine."

ACKNOWLEDGEMENTS

Some of these stories have previously appeared in magazines or contests: "A Sensitive Man Drinks Yellow Flowers" was an honourable mention in the 2024 Peter Hinchcliffe Fiction Prize and was subsequently published in *The New Quarterly*; "Hotel Viviane" was first published in *The New Quarterly*; "Chicken in Two Parts" was selected for admittance into the 2025 DISQUIET International Literary Program and previously published in *Prairie Fire*; "Raising James Dean" was longlisted for the 2025 DISQUIET Literary Fiction Contest; "We Should Change the Curtains" was a finalist in the Quebec Writers' Federation contest for emerging young writers and was published in *Soliloquies Anthology*; "The Milk's Gone Sour" in *The Link*. I am grateful to all the editors—Pamela Mulloy, Marjorie Poor, Celia Caldwell, and Marcus Bankuti—and grateful to Lori Schubert. An early version of this manuscript was submitted in partial fulfilment for the MA Creative Writing program at Concordia University. It won the David McKeen Award.

I am grateful to my editor, Dimitri Nasrallah, for your initial interest in the manuscript and subsequent guidance. I will take the whole process into the next book. I am also indebted to all the folks at Véhicule Press—Simon Dardick, Nancy Marrelli, and Jennifer Varkonyi—as well as to Mikhail Iossel, my thesis supervisor who helped shape an early version of this book, and has continued to provide guidance and kindness, and become a dear friend. Thank you to the Concordia writers and professors who helped along the way: Dimitri Nasrallah, Kate Sterns, Josip Novakovich, and Terence Byrnes. In no particular order, a tip of the hat to: Paige Cooper (for my earliest and most generous mentorship), Josh Quirion (for introducing me to an Italian audience), Jeremy Audet (for the voice notes, postcards, and 2027), Hilary Bergen (for bringing me back), Alexandre Marceau (for it all), Claire Russell (for setting me on the path), Robert Clooney (for the discovery), Braedan Houtman (for the dice), Katherine Abbass and Hannah Davis (for the comradery), Jonny Palucci (for Rimouski), Sean Lee (for the cigarettes and wine), Daniel Furlong (for the gasoline), and finally, the barista who sings at Pourquoi Pas espresso bar.

ESPLANADE
Books

A House by the Sea : A novel by Sikeena Karmali
A Short Journey by Car : Stories by Liam Durcan
Seventeen Tomatoes : Tales from Kashmir : Stories by Jaspreet Singh
Garbage Head : A novel by Christopher Willard
The Rent Collector : A novel by B. Glen Rotchin
Dead Man's Float : A novel by Nicholas Maes
Optique : Stories by Clayton Bailey
Out of Cleveland : Stories by Lolette Kuby
Pardon Our Monsters : Stories by Andrew Hood
Chef : A novel by Jaspreet Singh
Orfeo : A novel by Hans-Jürgen Greif
[Translated from the French by Fred A. Reed]
Anna's Shadow : A novel by David Manicom
Sundre : A novel by Christopher Willard
Animals : A novel by Don LePan
Writing Personals : A novel by Lolette Kuby
Niko : A novel by Dimitri Nasrallah
Stopping for Strangers : Stories by Daniel Griffin
The Love Monster : A novel by Missy Marston
A Message for the Emperor : A novel by Mark Frutkin
New Tab : A novel by Guillaume Morissette
Swing in the House : Stories by Anita Anand
Breathing Lessons : A novel by Andy Sinclair
Ex-Yu : Stories by Josip Novakovich
The Goddess of Fireflies : A novel by Geneviève Pettersen
[Translated from the French by Neil Smith]
All That Sang : A novella by Lydia Perović
Hungary-Hollywood Express : A novel by Éric Plamondon
[Translated from the French by Dimitri Nasrallah]
English is Not a Magic Language : A novel by Jacques Poulin
[Translated from the French by Sheila Fischman]
Tumbleweed : Stories by Josip Novakovich
A Three-Tiered Pastel Dream : Stories by Lesley Trites

Sun of a Distant Land : A novel by David Bouchet
[Translated from the French by Claire Holden Rothman]
The Original Face : A novel by Guillaume Morissette
The Bleeds : A novel by Dimitri Nasrallah
Nirliit : A novel by Juliana Léveillé-Trudel
[Translated from the French by Anita Anand]
The Deserters : A novel by Pamela Mulloy
Mayonnaise : A novel by Éric Plamondon
[Translated from the French by Dimitri Nasrallah]
The Teardown : A novel by David Homel
Apple S : A novel by Éric Plamondon
[Translated from the French by Dimitri Nasrallah]
Aphelia : A novel by Mikella Nicol
[Translated from the French by Lesley Trites]
Dominoes at the Crossroads : Stories by Kaie Kellough
Swallowed : A novel by Réjean Ducharme
[Translated from the French by Madeleine Stratford]
Book of Wings : A novel by Tawhida Tanya Evanson
The Geography of Pluto : A novel by Christopher DiRaddo
The Family Way : A novel by Christopher DiRaddo
Fear the Mirror : Stories by Cora Siré
Open Your Heart : A novel by Alexie Morin
[Translated from the French by Aimee Wall]
Hotline : A novel by Dimitri Nasrallah
Prophetess : A novel by Baharan Baniahmadi
A House Without Spirits : A novel by David Homel
Dandelion Daughter : A novel by Gabrielle Boulianne-Tremblay
[Translated from the French by Eli Tareq El Bechelany-Lynch]
Because : A novel by Andrew Steinmetz
Spirits in the Dark : A novel by H. Nigel Thomas
The War You Don't Hate : A novel by Blaise Ndala
[Translated from the French by Dimitri Nasrallah]
Kilworthy Tanner : A novel by Jean Marc Ah-Sen
Subterrane : A novel by Valérie Bah